GW00455901

THE SANDIE SHAW MYSTERIES

Book One

Murder at the Green Mill

R T GREEN

R T R G R E N

Other books...

The Daisy Morrow Series:

The Starstruck Series -

Starstruck: Somewhere to call Home
Starstruck: The Prequel
(Time to say Goodbye)
Starstruck: The Disappearance of Becca
Starstruck: The Rock
Starstruck: Ghosts, Ghouls and Evil Spirits
Starstruck: The Combo – books 1-3

The Raven Series –

Raven: No Angel!
Raven: Unstoppable
Raven: Black Rose
Raven: The Combo – books 1-3

Little Cloud
Timeless
Ballistic
Cry of an Angel
The Hand of Time
Wisp
The Standalones

COME AND JOIN US

We'd love you to become a VIP Reader.

Our intro library is the most generous in publishing!
Join our mail list and grab it all for free.
We really do appreciate every single one of you,
so there's always a freebie or two coming along,
news and updates, advance reads of new releases...

Go here to get started...
rtgreen.net

CONTENTS

Introduction

1920's Chicago. What came to be known as the 'roaring twenties'. For private investigator Sandie Shaw, 'roaring' was hardly the flattering kind of description she would ever give it.

Born and raised in the city, she despises everything it has become. In her view, Chicago typifies the false decadence gripping America. Only just recovering from the lawlessness of the days of the Wild West, her city and the rest of the country then entered the world war for a brief time, and when that was over, the whole nation seemed to lose all sense of reason.

People went crazy. Prohibition raised its ugly head, and the mobsters and the flappers took over Chicago. Her beloved city had fallen at the mercy of those who believed they were above the law... once again.

In all honesty, Chicago had long held the reputation of being the most lawless place in America. Prohibition, and corrupt governance, had handed a free ticket to the gangsters. It didn't sit well with Sandie.

Now fifty-three, for a long time she's had to be strong-willed to stay in one piece. Being gutsy and taking no nonsense helps to maintain a sense of right and wrong, and to retain her very individual identity. Much of Chicago in 1926 is wrong, but she does her best to stay on the right side of the worst of it. She doesn't break many laws, but those she does step outside of are small fry, and mostly because of her job.

Taking over the one-man agency when her father died, and making it a one-woman business, she knew from the off that in a male-dominated environment she would have to be tough, and witty, to succeed.

And that keeping well away from anyone with a machine gun was a big part of staying alive.

She managed it, for eight years refusing to be drawn into anything mob-related. But then one day someone comes to call, and without Sandie even realizing what she is getting into, suddenly she's up to her chin in murky waters.

And that changes everything...

Enjoy!
Richard and the crew

The Windy City

An incessant November rain bounced off the wide sidewalk of North Broadway, doing its best to head back the way it arrived. The massive drops jeweled the rainbow colours of the dazzling signs into a kaleidoscope of light that mirrored the dampness all around, trying to entice those who headed in their direction like flies to step inside for a never-to-be-forgotten evening.

Over on the other side of the road, a large queue of slightly-soggy people waited for the ornate doors of the Uptown Theatre to open, and allow them to escape the rain into the dry of its five-storey atrium. The place had made quite an impression since it opened the previous year, the punters loving the combination of spectacular live vaudeville, followed by movies.

A couple of doors down, on the corner of North Broadway and Lawrence, stood an establishment which had been there a while longer. The Green Mill had been around years before Prohibition, but since the insanity of the law banning liquor, had turned into what had become known as a Speakeasy.

Back in the day, I used to call in now and then, grabbing a whisky and a chat with Tom, the friendly owner. After prohibition I stopped going. Fruit juice with added illegal ingredients didn't really float my boat.

But that wasn't the real reason. When the bootleggers took over, and a hood called Jack McGurn supposedly became part-owner, neither Tom nor his establishment were the same. Not so much changed that anyone could see, except the clientele.

13

But behind closed doors, a lot more was going on. The trapdoor behind the bar that led to the cellar suddenly led to a lot more; secret tunnels to allow illicit liquor from Canada easy access from the lake, and the more infamous punters to escape if the need arose.

I shook my head as I threw a left into West Lawrence, walking quickly towards my office. Still I hadn't left the early-evening nightlife behind. Further down from the office was the Aragon Ballroom, and although it was only seven in the evening, men in Fedora hats and pin-stripe suits were escorting slender, scantily-clad flappers towards its doors.

I paused a moment, trying for the thousandth time to understand what my city had turned into. There were no sensible answers.

If I wanted to blame something, prohibition was top of the list.

Prohibition. For sure the most damaging law Congress ever passed. Ok, my live-and-let-live attitude was subject to certain limitations, but the Protestant do-gooders had easily exceeded those, on the basis of a pure logic they clearly couldn't see. If the government wanted to hand a free six-course meal ticket to the mobsters, that was the goddamn most sure-fire way to do it.

People had four staples in life. Air, water, food and liquor. The Temperance activists couldn't take the first three away, so they blamed the fourth for every problem America had. Somehow, against the odds, prohibition was born. The Chicago underworld lapped it up, and the liquor ban is currently responsible for a hell of a lot more problems than it's actually solving.

Problems like bringing one of our most unsavoury imports to the city. Our current most unsavoury resident, Johnny Torrio, invited him from New York, to be one of his lieutenants. Within weeks he was throwing his not-inconsiderable weight around, and when Torrio narrowly escaped death by bullet, and then decided he'd had enough, he gifted Al Capone control of his organization.

In a single year since that time, the man had changed the face of Chicago.

And if anything is more incredible that that, it's the fact that six years after it was first made law, prohibition is still going strong.

I turned the key in the dingy doorway that led directly off the sidewalk next to the Mexican food parlor I rented the upstairs floors from. Then I closed it behind me, and shut my eyes to try and ward off the depression that watching all the seemingly-oblivious good-time folks had forced into my mind.

The flappers insisted they were doing what they did for the right of women to be individuals. It hid a more basic fundamental reality. When their appearance and their flirty manner attracted the guys, they were just as vulnerable as any other girl. Machine guns, shiny jewelry, and false promises still ruled Chicago.

One day, when the unsustainable decadence and frivolity finally comes to an end, which it surely will, the flappers will disappear along with the rolls of banknotes, most of which were acquired in a less-than-legal manner.

As I opened my eyes again, and glanced up to the bare wooden steps leading to my office, I found my head shaking despondently once more. The smile on my face lacked any hint of humour as another thought entered my head. Chicago got the nickname the Windy City for one of two reasons. No one really knows which is true, but I'm pretty certain I do.

Some say it was because of the prairie winds that whipped along the roads from time to time. Some say it was because of the hot air emanating from those who were supposedly in control of the city.

"Vote for me, and I'll clean up this town..."

Yeah, right.

And my name is Calamity Jane.

———

Chapter 1

My shoes clunked up the echoic steps from the tiny lobby that led nowhere but the stairs. My legs seemed heavy, exhausted. It hadn't been the best of days, even leaving aside the depressing sight of the good-time guys and gals milling around outside.

I dragged my feet along the six feet of upper hallway to the opaque-glazed office door with my name etched into the glass, and slipped my key into the lock. It was already unlocked. I frowned, thinking the little guy who acted as my personal assistant had forgotten to lock it when he left.

As I walked in to the tiny lobby that pretended to be a reception area, I saw he was still there. He looked up, a little gratefully, but then pierced a blue eyed stare into me. 'Where have you been, Sandie? Been waiting for ages.'

'Waiting for what? You don't usually stick around after end of shift, Archie.'

He shook his ginger head. 'Well... um... you've got a visitor. So I had to wait.'

'A visitor? What kind of visitor?' I glanced through the opaque glass of the half-glazed door to my office. It seemed a bit foggy inside.

He looked slightly uncomfortable. Maybe that was an under-exaggeration. 'She arrived a couple of hours ago. I told her you might be ages, but she said she'd wait. She... um... seems to have been chain-smoking since she got here.'

'So I see... or not. Who is she?'

'Um... she wouldn't give the likes of me a name.'

'The likes of you? Who the hell does she think she is?'

'Well... she's a bit... impressive. In a well-heeled way, I mean.'

'So you don't know anything about her?'

Still he looked uncomfortable, like he'd recently come face to face with a lioness. 'She's... taller than me...'

'Everyone's taller than you, Archie.'

'No, I mean, a lot taller. And a little... haughty.'

'And she's *here?*'

'Well, yes. And she ain't going nowhere 'til she sees you, apparently.'

'I'm intrigued. Put your tongue away, it's not a good look.'

'My tongue isn't... ok, point taken.'

I sighed, a little wearily. 'Guess I'd better go see what she wants. Last thing I need right now.'

He looked at me, a little sympathetically. 'The Mendes job didn't go so well, then?'

'Put it like this, Archie. A short while ago I left Joachim, after telling him the wife he thought was having an affair was indeed seeing another man... a Latin dance instructor, and a goddamn better looking guy than he is.'

'Aw, but I guess that's a result then?'

'Not really. Turns out all she was doing actually *was* having lessons, in secret, so she could ask her husband to take her to the Aragon for their tenth anniversary, and not let him down on the dance floor.'

'Ouch. He must have been relieved though, finding out his wife *wasn't* having an affair?'

'He might have been, if I hadn't messed up.'

'What, you?'

'I'll ignore that, seeing as you're just the insignificant little squirt who works for me.'

'Point taken. Go on...'

18

'They caught me taking pictures of them, so I could show Mr. Mendes the truth. Mrs. Mendes wasn't too happy when I had to explain, as you can imagine. And neither was her husband, when I reported back what had happened.'

'Double ouch.'

'You could say. He shook his head, and handed me the twenty dollar fee anyway. I told him to put it back in his pocket, and brace himself for when his wife got home.'

'Triple ouch. All that and no pay.'

I threw my hands in the air, trying to express how helpless I felt. 'What could I do? He was gonna need a lot more than that to keep his marriage in one piece.'

'For sure. Not the best of days then.'

'Prairie pig of a day, and it's left a lousy taste in my mouth. Neither of them deserved that.'

'And now you gotta go see what the Amazonian wants.'

'Tell me about it. Go home, Archie. I'll see if I can get rid of her, and then hit the illegal whisky.'

The office was a haze of smoke as I walked in. I could just about make out the shape of a well-dressed woman sitting in my chair behind the desk, a packet of cigarettes on its top.

In no mood for foggy offices, I headed straight for the outside wall. 'Geez, can't you open a window?'

The husky voice didn't seem fazed by my irreverence. 'It's November. And anyway, the advertising says if I smoke Lucky Strikes, I stay slim.'

I threw open the single window, and heard the sound of the heavy rain suddenly get louder as the chilly but fresh air penetrated the fog. I had to shoot down the woman's nonsense. 'My husband is a heart and lung surgeon, and he says the only way smoking Lucky Strikes keeps you slim is by making you ill.'

'Really.'

'Nah, not really. Just making a point.'

The woman stood up and vacated my seat as the fog began to clear, and held out a hand. 'Anyway, we talk of irrelevancies. My name is Daphne deMountford. Pleased to make your acquaintance.'

Chapter 2

I took the elegant lace-clad hand, and looked her over. She seemed to thunder into my brain in sections.

First it was the short black fringed bob, the style favoured by both the flappers and the well-heeled. Then the perfect white smile, her full lips framed by red lipstick, dazzling me from out of a brown face.

Then I noticed the long sable-coloured coat, its hems and collar trimmed with fox-fur that was clearly real, hanging open to reveal a sheer multi-coloured dress that seemed to cling to every slender but shapely shape she possessed.

Then came the legs, their flawless brown skin having no need for stockings. The goddamn things seemed to go right up to her chin, emphasized by shoes with three-inch red heels, that again she didn't really need, taking her overall height to what must have been six feet.

I swallowed hard, trying not to let her see I had. 'Pleased to meet you too, Mrs. deMountford,' I said as steadily as I could. No one really fazed me these days, but for some reason, she surely did.

She sat down elegantly in the seat on the other side of the desk, and took a long draw from the cigarette in the holder between her slender fingers. 'Please, it's Daphne... deMountford is so... English. I realize it is late, and I apologize for keeping your man-friday from his evening. He seems a little... little.'

'Archie? He's a gem. And he works for peanuts.'

She cast her eyes around her not-very-salubrious surroundings. 'Forgive me, but I can't imagine you can afford to pay him very much anyway.'

'No I mean, he works for peanuts... literally. He's got an addiction to them.'

'Really?'

'Well, kind of. I do let him have a little cash on good days.'

She lowered her head, and hesitated a moment, like she didn't want to say the words. 'I needed to talk with you about something that is disturbing me.'

I opened my mouth to say words along the lines of being surprised anything could disturb her, but decided against it. Instead I said something equally inane. 'Sure. I'm a little surprised though. I don't get many AA's in this office.'

She frowned. 'AA's?'

I realized as soon as the words left my lips it was almost as idiotic as what I'd originally intended to say, so tried to bumble my way through an explanation. 'Sorry, I didn't mean any disrespect. AA is private investigator speak for African-Americans... MX for Mexicans, GM for Germans, Iti's for Italians, that kind of thing. It saves time when you're writing up notes.'

'I see. And what is the abbreviation for Chicago natives?'

'Um... there isn't one. We don't get many of those.'

'Then perhaps I have come to the right place. You were the only female private investigator I could find. The... situation is a little bit delicate, and I didn't want an untrustworthy man involved.'

'And what makes you think I'm any more trustworthy?'

'You're a woman, aren't you?'

'Last time I looked. Thank you.'

She shook her head. That seemed elegant too. 'Don't thank me. You don't know what I want you to do yet.'

'That's true. But you still surprise me. We don't get many people of your... status in here either.'

'I see your private eyes have already led you to assume my standing in life.'

'Um... it is a little obvious, if you don't mind me saying.'

'Not at all. In England my husband was a lord, with ancestral ties to the royal family.'

'*Was?* Surely once a lord, always a lord?'

'Not if you're stripped of your title, no.'

'I see. Well, I don't. Perhaps you should explain?'

For the first time she looked borderline uncomfortable. Or what passed for it, given her elegant everything. 'My parents moved to England from Ghana when I was a child. I met James... Mr. deMountford, when I worked as a servant at a function he was attending. To cut a long story short, we were attracted to each other, and began a secret relationship. After a while the newspapers started publishing speculative articles, which of course came to the attention of the royal family.'

'Never did like George very much.'

'I said we should end the relationship, but James refused. He stood his ground, but he was up against the entire English aristocracy, who took no prisoners. He said most of them were just jealous.'

I nodded, even though I really didn't want to. 'He was probably right.'

She lowered her head. 'It didn't really matter. He was ostracized, so we emigrated to America. On the Titanic, as it happens.'

'Oh my god... you obviously survived.'

'Indeed. Not exactly the ideal start to our new life. James had studied at Cambridge, so he became a bookkeeper... not because he had to, he managed to slip away with some of his fortune, but because he wanted to work, to be a normal man, I suppose. He made a success of himself, while we lived in New York. Then, a year ago, we moved here.'

'Geez, what attracted you to this mob-infested place?'

She glanced up to me. 'You surprise me. I would have thought with all the gangsters roaming around, and your line of work, you would have many clients amongst them?'

'Hell no. The mob tends to sort out their own problems... but in truth, if anyone came through that door whiffing of hood, I'd send them packing straightaway. Not interested, in any shape or form.'

'I see.'

'So, you and James had a relationship made in heaven, and a small fortune to back you up... so just what is the problem you're here about?'

Again she looked a little squirmy. 'Perhaps it was a bad idea coming here.'

'Hey. You sit waiting for two hours, stop my valued assistant from going home, while all the time polluting my office with smoke... the least you can do is tell me why you came.'

'I think James is having an affair.'

'Ok... sure didn't see that one coming.'

Chapter 3

An awkward silence fell over the room, so I decided I had to be the one to break it. 'On what grounds do you believe he's seeing someone else?'

She didn't answer for a moment, looking uncomfortable at the possibility of revealing facts she likely thought she'd never have to. 'James and I know each other extremely well... inside out, you might say... so when someone you know that well starts acting out of character, you notice.'

'Ok, so give me a few actual facts.'

'He... just lately he's been... disconnected. Like there's something on his mind. I tackled him about it, but he just smiled and told me I was worrying about nothing.'

'Perhaps you are worrying about nothing.'

'I tried to tell myself that. But he's lost his smile, and seems preoccupied...'

'It doesn't mean he's having an affair.'

'Not on its own, no. But a couple of times lately he's made excuses, saying he had to work into the evening. The second time I phoned him at the office to ask what time he'd be home. Some cleaning woman answered, said no one was there.'

'Maybe he was working somewhere else. Did you confront him about it?'

She shook her head. 'No. When he got home I asked him if it was relaxing, working in the office when no one else was in the building. He said it was, and that he might have to do it a few more times. He lied to me, Sandie.'

'Ok, so it kinda smacks of guilt.'

She nodded, and took an overly-long suck on the cigarette holder. It was clear she didn't want to be doing what she was, and it wasn't sitting easy. Again I was the one to break the awkwardness. 'What do you want me to do, if I accept the assignment?'

'I suppose... the next time he says he's working late, follow him and see where he goes... or something? Whatever it is you private investigators do.'

'I'm not sure, Daphne. Yeah, I could do with the work, but there's only your suspicious mind to go on. I think I might need a little more than that.'

She reached into her beaded snake-skin reticule, pulled out an envelope, and tossed it onto the desktop in front of me. 'Then allow me to give you more.'

I looked inside the envelope, and couldn't help raising my eyebrows, even though I tried not to. 'A hundred dollars?'

'If you succeed, and tell me what I need to know, you will be paid the same again.'

'Wow, you must be desperate, spending two hundred dollars of your money on a feeling.'

She smiled, dazzling me again. 'Oh, it's not *my* money.'

'Then who's is it?'

'Why, James's of course.'

'*Really?* You want me to spy on your husband, and get *him* to pay for it?'

'Oh, he'll never miss it. And what price peace of mind, hey?'

'Well, that's one way of dealing the cards, I guess.'

'That is the way I choose to look at it, Sandie. So will you do as I ask?'

My eyes fell to the envelope. It was tempting, a lot of money for a female private investigator who usually had to pick up the crumbs her male counterparts left behind. 'I guess...'

'Good.' She stood up, her black bob, which was most likely a wig, close to the not-very-high ceiling. 'The very next time my husband says he has to work late, I will telephone you. Perhaps if I could have your number?'

I hadn't actually said a definitive yes, despite the obvious benefits. But the Amazonian Daphne had eagerly assumed I had, and it was a lot of money after all. It was obvious it had been extremely hard for her to even come to see me, something borne out by the fact she'd waited so long for me to get back to the office.

She was likely well aware if she'd left without spilling her guts to me, she may never have found the courage to come again. I handed her my card, and tried to smile reassuringly, as much for me as for her.

She was a fellow woman after all. And she was clearly cut up about the direction her life was taking. She and I were worlds apart in so many ways, and yet I still found myself feeling sympathy with her dilemma, and a grudging admiration for the fact she'd found the strength to even be in my office.

I promised her I would do all I could to set her mind at rest, or not, as the case may turn out to be. But I had to remind her there were no promises of definitive results.

She nodded, shook my hand, and left. I watched her walk quickly down the stairs, feeling a little like I was cheating her, even though it wasn't actually her money paying me. In the world I moved in, it was a large fee for what could be just one night's work, if James deMountford did the right things... or the wrong things, depending on which pair of eyes you looked at it with.

I locked the office door, a little voice in the back of my head wondering what I was getting myself into. As I headed up the second set of stairs to my tiny apartment on the top floor, I knew the only way to find out was to get myself into it.

Had I known then what I knew a week later, I would have shown Daphne deMountford the door straightaway, before she'd even had chance to take another fog-inducing draw on her cigarette holder.

But right then, I had no idea it was anything other than just another unfaithful-partner job.

Chapter 4

Gut feelings are hard to define. Hell, it's hard enough to know if they even exist or not. But as I sat on the slightly flea-bitten sofa in my slightly flea-bitten apartment, sipping a glass of real whisky, they sure seemed to exist right then.

The whisky was an under-the-counter gift from a grateful client. God only knows where he got it from, but somehow it had made its way across the pond, all the way from Scotland. It sure beat the fake crap they peddled in the speakeasies these days. It was my occasional go-to comfort blanket, when the gut feelings depressed the hell out of me.

Like the feeling something massive was going to happen to kill the decadence and the frivolity of the flappers, and their brazen approach to life. Maybe not this year, maybe not next, but sooner or later some kind of drastic event would transpire to bring the current unsustainable era to an abrupt end.

I'm not a killjoy. Ok, I may be too old to be a flapper, but it was the last thing I wanted to be anyway. I like a bit of fun, even though there's no one in my life to share it with. But putting yourself out there to attract the right kind of rich man was a risky business in Chicago.

You were just as likely to attract the wrong kind of rich man, and get drawn into the seedier side of city life.

Daphne deMountford had a gut feeling too. One that seemed to be dominating my thoughts. She never dreamt she'd be thinking the kind of things she was, and even though she was doing her damndest to hide it, her gut feeling was eating away at her.

An African-American who most people viewed as unfairly living above her station in life, she couldn't have many friends of her own in Chicago. Those she knew were almost certainly 'friends' of her husband. If he was being unfaithful, and that subsequently resulted in a break-up, those so-called friends would instantly side with James.

She was far from stupid. She knew that harsh fact of life too. If her gut feeling proved correct, she would be ostracized, and suddenly find herself alone. It wasn't a nice place to be. From what my gut was telling me, they'd both done what they had for love. Which might turn out to be a bad move for her.

If I discovered what could likely be a vindication of her gut, I might end up being all she had left.

I shook my head, emptied the glass, and headed to bed to try and dream of more pleasant things. They say if you have a conscience, you shouldn't be a private investigator unless you can separate it from your working life.

Somehow I never could. But that's just tough.

Just after lunchtime the next day, I did something I hadn't done for three years. I visited the Green Mill.

I don't know why. Actually seeing what it had become was likely to be as depressing as most other things these days. But my mind was still full of the immensely-tall Daphne, so maybe I needed an equally disturbing distraction to rid my mind of her.

And at that time of day it was unlikely any of the bar's more unpleasant punters would be there anyway.

I was virtually alone as I walked through the side door. The Mill didn't *really* open during the day, except for its own variation of coffee... it came alive, in all kinds of ways, after darkness fell. But it wasn't really closed either, from lunchtime onwards.

I saw just one couple, sitting in the booth I'd been told was Al Capone's favourite. It was the only one that had a view of both entrance doors, so he and his men could see danger approaching the moment it did. Whether that was from a rival gang or from a half-hearted token police raid, it wasn't clear.

As I walked up to the huge mahogany bar top, which looked about as thick as the length of my forearm, I noticed the trapdoor in the floor behind it was open. Tom was likely down in the cellar, busy restocking his above and below-the-counter wares. While I waited for him to reappear, I took my own visual stock of the place.

Not much seemed to have changed in three years. At least, not on the surface. The crazily-long bar top, which curved at one end, still dominated the left side of the room. Joe E Lewis's band were busy setting up on the low stage at the head of the room, and the statue of Ceres still stood proudly on her pedestal in the far corner.

The murals still dominated the upper half of the walls, shrouded by ornate-shaped frames. The curved booths still lined the bottom half, leaving enough floor room for those who wished to dance the night away to the live jazz... not that there was much space for frivolities like dancing when the room got full.

The Mill was a fraction of the size it was four years ago. Before Tom sold much of it off to what is now the Uptown Theatre, it had large sunken gardens, where guests could hold functions, and mooch away their celebrations in the Chicago moonlight.

It was quite a place back then, before the mobsters and vaudeville took hold. Now, despite the fact the gangsters were making it the place to be seen once again, somehow it just wasn't the same.

Tom's head appeared from beneath the floor. 'Well, here's a thing. The honourable Sandie Shaw, finally gracing us with her presence after, what... three years?'

I grinned. 'I must have made an impression, Tom, if you remember how long it's been.'

'Part of my job, Sandie.' He leant over, and we gave each other a hug.

'How have you been, Tom?' I asked, genuinely concerned. He looked alright enough, but bar owners often did, whether they were or not.

'Well, y'know, Sandie.'

'Actually I don't. Maybe you should tell me?'

He lifted his hands from his sides, in a resigned kind of way. 'Business changes, y'know. Especially for bar owners.'

I found my eyes narrowing, all on their own. 'You mean speakeasy owners.'

'If you like.'

'I stopped coming because it just wasn't the same, Tom. I prefer to keep my distance from the mob.'

He looked a little furtive, just for a moment. 'Keep your voice down, Sandie. A couple of them are down below, overseeing the... latest deliveries.'

'Booze made from engine oil, you mean.'

'Hey, that's a little unkind. Ok, but it works. Folks pull a face at the first shot, but then they ask for a second. By the sixth, they can't get enough. That's good business for me, in these times.'

'That's sad business, Tom.'

'Yeah well, like I have a choice.'

'You could have held out on them... but then no one else does, so why should you?'

'No flies on you, huh?'

'I hear you're just taking on a partner, so someone must think it's worth it.'

'Don't believe everything you hear, Sandie.' I raised my eyebrows, so he shook his head. 'So Mr. Capone, he's taken a fancy to the place. That brings in the punters, and now I don't have to pay no protection, if you get me.'

'*Mr. Capone?* Such respect, Tom.'

'Not something you seem to suffer from. And keep it that way, as long as you can. So why are you here, anyway?' he asked, hastily changing the subject.

'Aw, you know, just a change of scene from one depressing vista to another.'

He grinned. 'You wanna drink?'

'Sure. As long as it's not engine oil.'

He reached somewhere below the counter, slid a secret compartment aside, pulled out a bottle of real gin, and poured me a large shot. 'So why are you here, anyway?' he repeated himself.

'Got me a case, and it's making my gut grumble. Just don't ask me why, coz I don't know.'

'Geez... not mob-related?'

'Nah... rich dude related.'

He laughed. 'You telling me you're nervous because of rich pickings?' he asked incredulously.

'I told you, I don't know why I'm nervous. I just needed a few minutes of distraction.'

'That's the trouble with gut feelings. They ain't specific enough.'

'Tell me about it.'

'Tell *me* about it?'

I sighed. Up until three years ago Tom had been my sounding board. Now, it looked like he was about to be again. 'Yesterday, someone came to see me. A woman, with a possible infidelity case. Don't ask me why, but that little voice in the back of my head is telling me to be careful.'

'A woman? Kindred spirits then, surely?'

'Maybe. But we couldn't be more different. She's AA, ten feet tall, and… impressive, according to Archie.'

He frowned. 'She got a name?'

'Daphne deMountford.'

He whistled, and shook his head. 'Geez… the African Queen?'

My eyebrows shot into the air, genuinely this time. 'You know her?'

'Only because she and that husband of hers come in here sometimes. She's…'

A head appearing at the trapdoor, and the curt shout emanating from it, interrupted whatever he was about to say to me. *'Hey, Tom… we getting any help down here, or what?'*

Suddenly he looked like a frightened rabbit. 'Sandie, I gotta go. Just be careful, ok?'

The head poking out of the trapdoor disappeared again. I thought I recognized the face from the papers. 'Is that Machine Gun McGurn, without his machine gun?'

'One and the same. Take care, Sandie.'

He was gone. I finished my drink, left a dollar bill on the counter, and walked back to the office, just as depressed as when I first left it. The things Tom said, and didn't say, had answered a few questions I didn't know I was asking, but the one thing he hadn't had the chance to say might have told me more.

I headed back up the stairs, the feeling in my gut turning into a butterfly boxing match. Not knowing why it was there wasn't helping… again.

34

Chapter 5

Archie grinned, inanely as usual, as I walked into the tiny reception. 'Good drink?'

'The drink was, yeah. The rest of it was just as depressing as this hellhole.'

He ran a hand through his ginger locks. 'Aw, not sure I should pass on the news if you're in this mood then.'

He made me smile, as he often did. 'Just tell me, Peanut. It can't be any worse.'

'You had a phone call. That Amazon woman.'

My stomach did a somersault, even though I tried to stop it mid-way. 'Quit with calling her an Amazon woman. She's African.'

'As you wish... Mrs. deMountford called to speak with you,' he intonated in proper English.

'Ok, now you're just making a point. What did she want?'

I kind of already knew, but Archie's words confirmed it anyway. 'She wouldn't say. Asked that you call her back as soon as possible.'

He handed me a slip of paper with her number on it. 'Thanks, Archie,' I said, almost reluctantly. 'I'll call her from the office.'

I slumped wearily into the chair behind my desk, and dialed the number. A voice I didn't know answered.

'Good afternoon. The deMountford residence.'

'May I speak to Daphne please?'

'Just a moment. Who is calling?'

I told her who I was, and there was silence for a minute. *'Sandie... thank you for calling back. Wait a second...'*

Again there was silence, while Daphne made sure she was alone. *'James called, a little while ago. Said he had to work late again. I think this may be our opportunity.'*

She sounded afraid, like she really didn't want to part with the information. Again, although I tried not to let it, my heart went out to her. 'Ok Daphne, do you want me to follow him, see where he goes?'

'Can I come and see you, now?'

'Sure, but there's no need, unless you want to.'

'I would like to. One hour.'

She killed the call. I sat back, unsure if wanting to see me was because she didn't wish to talk on the phone, or if it was for another reason.

I saw the Model T taxi arrive. Maybe I was watching out of the window, perhaps it was just coincidence. She paid the driver, and walked elegantly to my door. Wearing a long red coat with black fur this time, she still looked every bit the statuesque Amazonian that Archie seemed to like to describe her as.

A minute later she was walking through my door, cigarette holder in hand straightaway. I'd already opened the window, in anticipation.

'Thank you for seeing me,' she said, throwing me the dazzling but slightly unsure smile as she lit up. 'I... I'm not sure why I came though.'

'Maybe you just needed a little girl time.'

'Perhaps.'

'So do you want me to follow him, see where he goes?' I asked again.

'I... I suppose I do, if that's ok.'

'It's really your call. You've already paid me a large sum of his money. I think we both need to know, don't you?'

The voice hesitated a moment. 'Yes, although it's not sitting easily.'

'That's obvious by your tone, and not exactly surprising. But knowing is better than not knowing. It might all be perfectly innocent.' I found myself trying to reassure her, even though I didn't believe for one second it was innocent. 'Are you ok?'

She shook her head. 'Not really. I feel dirty, and sitting at home staring at the walls isn't helping.'

'I take it you don't work?'

She shook her head. 'Not at the moment. Back in New York I trained to be a dancer and actress, and when we arrived in Chicago I got a job in a vaudeville production. But after two weeks they fired me.'

'Why did they do that? Were you a crap dancer?'

My irrelevance made her smile. 'The official line was that I was too tall, and it made the other chorus girls look silly.'

'But?'

'The director whispered in my ear it was because they'd had a few complaints from well-heeled punters they didn't want to be watching a black face.'

'I doubt it was your face they were watching.'

'Whichever bit, it was still black.'

'Geez… small-minded bastards. I'm so sorry.'

'Thank you. After that I auditioned for the new play that premieres next month, for the role of Mama Morton, but it was the same again. They didn't want a black actress in the role.'

'You're talking about *Chicago*, written by that sensationalist Tribune reporter Maurine Dallas Watkins?'

'She's not a reporter anymore, now her play is about to hit the big time. I'm surprised you've heard of it.'

'Everyone in Chicago has heard of it. She called the main character Roxie Hart, didn't she?'

'Yes. I think perhaps it will be a smash.'

'Yeah. There'll be a movie or two, no doubt.'

'I suppose it is a possibility.'

My heart went out to her, again. 'I'm sorry, Daphne. Being a rich, black Englishwoman living in Chicago can't be easy.'

She sucked a long draw from the cigarette, and glanced up to the ceiling. I swear there was a little mistiness in her eyes. 'No, it isn't. Having money becomes a burden after a while, so my only joy is James, and now...'

'Hey, all hope is not lost. He might actually be working late. But tonight we find out for sure, ok?'

She nodded. 'One way or another.'

I tried to draw her away to practicalities. 'I'll need to know what he looks like, and where his office is.'

'Yes, it's in a downtown building. He rents an office on the fourth floor. I've written down the address.'

I took the photograph and the address she handed me. He looked every inch the handsome English aristocrat, and it was easy to see what the attraction was for a Ghanaian servant girl. And looking at the woman sitting a few feet away, easy to see what the benefits were from his perspective, if you didn't possess an archaic bias against black skin.

I would have to follow him right from his office, and see where he went. After that... well, it depended *where* he went.

'Ok Daphne, try and be as normal as you can when he gets back. If it's late, maybe pretend to be asleep, even if you're not. If there's time before he makes it home, I'll call you later tonight. If there isn't, it'll be first thing in the morning.'

'Please don't let him see you. I don't need photographs or anything, your word is good enough for me.'

'Ok, thanks. I'll be careful, I promise.'

Daphne left, and I sat back and closed my eyes. She'd talked like a reluctant arch-criminal, but the hesitation she was feeling wasn't justified. James deMountford was up to something, and he was keeping whatever it was from the woman he supposedly never kept anything from.

She had every right to know what that was. He might have the best reasons in the world for keeping it to himself, but he was still telling lies. At the end of the day, it was far better for everyone to know why.

Especially the both of us.

Somehow the job for Daphne I'd kind of accepted wasn't really much different from most of the work I normally carried out. But it was getting to me. Deep inside my head I was worried about something, but no matter how hard I tried, I couldn't latch onto what it was.

Don't get personally involved, my father had said before he handed over the business. For eight years I'd kept that faith, but this time I realized I was slipping. And no matter what I did, I couldn't seem to gain a foothold to climb back to indifference.

Maybe it was because my last job ended up a dismal failure. Maybe it was because a seemingly-perfect marriage had sprung a leak, and I wanted to prove to myself I could plug it once and for all.

For Daphne's sake. For my own peace of mind's sake.

There wasn't much peace in either of our minds right then. The logistics of the job were simple enough. I knew

39

James's office building, and the fact that apart from the fire escape, there was only one entrance and exit. Once he left, an experienced investigator like me could follow him, and not let him realize I was... especially when a camera wasn't involved.

But for some unfathomable reason, I needed to see where he went in the hope I could report back his dalliance was totally innocent. Having to tell Daphne he was seeing someone else was scaring the hell out of me.

Right at that moment, that was the most baffling thing of all.

I guess if I'd listened to my sense of reason instead of my heart, I would have heard different things. Like the fact the two of them had only arrived in Chicago just over a year ago, and the even more telling fact Tom at the Green Mill knew they existed.

If I had listened to practicalities, I would have realized Daphne wasn't telling me everything. Not because she didn't want to, but because she knew if she had, I would have shown her the door.

I didn't know it, but my trip out this evening was the point of no return. Once I discovered where James was going, there would be no turning back.

For either of us.

Chapter 6

The rain had stopped, but the improvement in the weather didn't seem to reflect in my mood. As I reached James's office building, the awful feeling of impending doom wasn't going away.

It wasn't very far from my own office, so I walked the few blocks, and took up position by a small taxi rank on the opposite side of the road from the main entrance. It was five-forty-five, and it seemed like a million people were whizzing around like ants, most of them likely heading home from work. My mark's normal finishing time was six, so if he kept to that but headed somewhere else other than home, I was in the right place at the right time.

The taxi rank was a bonus too. It was hardly unusual for there to be someone waiting around, so I didn't stand out. Plus, if James took a taxi instead of walking somewhere, it would be a simple matter for me to do the same, and call to the driver to *'Follow that cab!'*

There was no way to know how he would get to wherever he was going, until he actually went.

My eyes inadvertently lifted to the fourth floor of the building. There were only five floors anyway, and a few windows were already dark. Occupied mostly by lawyers and bookkeepers, neither of those professions tended to work late unless they were forced to.

Lights were still shining from a couple of square windows on the fourth floor. Daphne didn't know if his office was located at the front or the back, so it was impossible to tell if one of them was his. I kept one of my eyes on the brightly-lit entrance, and a couple of times I thought I saw him leave, but after a little eye-narrowing, realized neither of the leavers was him.

Damn Fedora hats... from a certain distance, a lot of decent-looking men seemed identical. And in the kind of professional workplace James occupied, looking similar was considered essential.

It wasn't helping. But at least it wasn't raining.

It was cold though. The raw Chicago winter was fast approaching, so I wrapped my woolly scarf tighter around my neck, and hoped my mark wouldn't be too long.

Someone answered my prayers. Three minutes later a man walked out of the main doors, and looked like the mark who would allow my body to move. Still I couldn't be sure, but that baffling gut feeling was telling me it was him.

For a second he glanced to the right and the left, and then set off along the sidewalk, heading south. He was keeping close to the building, but trying not to be too noticeable. Something about his manner told me he was my man.

I crossed the road to follow him, but the mass of cars and scurrying people didn't make that as easy as I'd envisaged. Trying to keep an eye out for my life, and another on the mark, didn't prove to be ideal. As I reached the opposite side of the road, he'd disappeared into the crowd.

I growled something unrepeatable to myself. All I could do was get to the last place I knew he'd been. I joined the scurrying masses, and made it to the last point I'd seen him.

It was the corner of the block. There were four ways he could have gone. I came to a stop, trying to think logically. Three of those ways involved crossing insanely-busy roads. The chances were he would still be waiting for traffic, or at

42

least have only just reached the other side. There was no sign of him.

The law of averages would say he'd not crossed a road, which meant there was only one option. I had no choice, I did what he'd likely done and turned right, praying to the god of private investigators it was the right move.

It was the right move. The sea of bobbing Fedoras was a little quieter there, and I spotted him. I breathed a sigh of intense relief. Reporting back that I'd lost my mark within thirty seconds of locating him would not look good on the resume. And it wouldn't sit well with me or my client.

He was walking like he was simply heading home, just in the wrong direction. In his left hand, a brown leather briefcase made me wish I possessed x-ray vision. He was likely carrying it simply to disguise the underhand purpose of his journey, but it might still contain something relevant.

He was giving nothing away, so there was no choice but to complete my task, and follow him to see where he went. I didn't have to wait long to find out, but the place he finally stopped wasn't anywhere near where I expected my journey to end.

He walked nonchalantly up the three steps to a small bank. I narrowed my eyes as I sidled into a doorway a few doors down that gave me a view of the bank's entrance. The place had closed over an hour earlier, and the interior was almost dark, bathed in just the dim night-light of the security guard's lamp.

Was James going to wait for someone outside the bank, a pre-arranged meeting place?

It seemed my thought was wrong. His free hand reached up to the bell-pull, and a minute later someone unlocked and opened the door. That someone sure didn't look like anyone he was having an affair with; dressed in a not-inexpensive suit, he looked like the manager, or someone very high up in the bank's hierarchy.

They shook hands, and disappeared inside. The door was locked behind them.

What the hell? I watched for a moment to see if anything else transpired. All was quiet, so then I threw my eyes to the dark sky, and asked myself what to do next.

It wasn't easy to know. What I'd seen wasn't simple to explain. Perhaps the bank was where he kept his fortune, but bank managers weren't in the habit of opening up after hours, even for their well-heeled customers. The manager in question clearly knew James was visiting, and the smiles and handshakes were a clear indication they were familiar with each other, and the after-hours dalliance likely not the first of its kind.

What were they up to? Daphne might be able to shed some light, but that was a definite maybe. She would however know where their fortune was located. If it was the same bank, then it would explain a few things.

It wouldn't explain everything though. Like what James was actually doing there, having clearly organized an after-hours meeting with someone very high-up... and likely not for the first time. Or why he was doing whatever it was without telling his wife, and lying to her to cover his tracks.

The one redeeming fact was that it looked pretty certain he wasn't having an affair... unless it was a threesome with the manager and a secretary. Somehow, a highly unlikely scenario.

So just what was going on? Without talking with Daphne, there was no light to shed right then. I decided to wait a while, to see how long James was inside. It would very likely freeze my tits off, but hanging around might tell me a little more to help unearth the truth.

Luckily for my extremities, I didn't have long to wait. Fifteen minutes after James went into the bank, he was shaking hands with the manager again, and walking away.

Towards me. I turned to the door in my borrowed entranceway, and pretended to stick a fictitious key in the lock, like I was just leaving. He passed right by me, and didn't give me a second glance. I left it a few seconds, and followed him.

The briefcase was still in his hand, just like before. Frustratingly, there was nothing to say if he'd taken something to the bank, or collected something from it.

He headed back to the street where his office was located, but then crossed the road to the taxi rank. The crowds had thinned, most of the massing throngs already home, and the night-life not yet beginning. I quickened my step, and almost caught up with him. I heard his clipped English tones, asking the driver if he could take him somewhere.

The driver nodded, and James got into the taxi. I nodded too, metaphorically. I knew where the deMountford's lived, and where the vehicle was heading. They were one and the same.

Whatever mysterious thing he'd been doing, James wasn't doing it anymore. He was going home to his wife.

Chapter 7

There was no chance to call Daphne. I cast my eyes around the street, but could see no telephone booths in sight. There would be one not so far away, and it might take a while for James to get home in the traffic. It likely wouldn't be so long though, the traffic lighter then, and the taxi driver keen to get back for the lucrative nightlife work.

It was too risky to phone her, and apart from that I had a few questions to ask, which might mean the call was a lengthy one. It was better left until morning. I needed a little time to think about what to say to her anyway.

I headed back to my apartment. I wanted to walk quickly, a freezing wind whipping around my legs, but somehow they didn't want to move very fast. The contradictory thoughts bouncing around my head might be something to do with the lack of speed-walking.

I could reassure Daphne of her husband's fidelity. It still wasn't conclusive he truly wasn't seeing someone, but from what I'd observed I got the feeling it was hardly the first time he'd had a secret meeting with someone who didn't appear to be another woman.

On the other side of the coin was the fact that in quelling her fears, I had opened up another potential can of worms. James's actions might have been innocent, but banks didn't meet clients after hours unless there was a very good reason. To someone with my suspicious nature, that meant Daphne might have more to worry about than infidelity.

It also meant I had more to worry about. Sure, I could pocket the other half of my lucrative fee, and rid my life of my chain-smoking Amazonian client. But unanswered questions tended to fester in my mind, and had a habit of not being cured by a few shots of whisky, real or otherwise.

And when all was said and done, what I'd seen tonight might eventually mean that Daphne would end up alone after all.

As I stuck my key in the apartment door, I shook my head to try and rid it of the thoughts that seemed to be spinning in ever decreasing circles. I told myself I was over-thinking again, creating scenarios that weren't really there.

But somehow, I still couldn't extricate myself from the bad feeling.

'Sorry I couldn't call last night... James was already heading home, earlier than I think we both expected.'

Daphne didn't reply straightaway, likely summoning up the strength to ask the million-dollar question. *'Did... did you find anything out, Sandie?'*

'Yes. He's not having an affair. At least, he wasn't last night.'

I actually heard the sigh of relief. *'Oh, thank god. I... I need to bring you the rest of the fee.'*

'I'd like to see you anyway. I have a few questions.'
'Questions?'

'Where he went was certainly not anywhere men go to meet another woman. But it raises... look, can you come, so we can talk in private?'

'I was going to suggest I call in, bring you the cash. Sandie, what's this about?'

She sounded unsure, wary. I had to try and ease her mind. 'Look Daphne, James is innocent of infidelity, but I just need to ask you a couple of things so I can put the case to bed. Will you come as soon as you can, please?'

'I'll be on my way in five minutes.'

47

She walked into the office with the dazzling smile, which looked a little brighter than before. I'd opened the window, but there was no sign of the cigarette holder. She sat down confidently in the chair on the other side of the desk, and slapped an envelope onto its top.

'There you go. The balance of your fee. Thank you so much, Sandie.'

I didn't pick up the envelope. *'Daphne...'*

She looked at me curiously. 'Is my newfound joy somewhat premature?'

'No... well, maybe. Oh, don't get me wrong, James doesn't appear to be seeing anyone else. So on that one, I can set your mind at rest.'

'Then why the long face, and the awkward hesitation?'

'Because... Daphne, which bank did you withdraw this from?'

'I didn't. We keep some cash for expenses in a safe at home. James never wants me to run out of funds.'

My eyebrows raised, all by themselves. 'And he never asks questions?'

She shook her head. 'He trusts me... even when he perhaps shouldn't.'

This time it was my head shaking. 'Ok, so which bank is your fortune kept in?'

She gave me the dazzle again. 'Why, Sandie... have I not paid you enough?'

'No... I mean yes... the fee is very generous. I just need to ask.'

A frown puckered her perfect brow. 'Since we have been in the city, our somewhat-diminished fortune is in the Chicago State Bank, which is also where James's current income is placed. Please tell me why you ask.'

48

It was my turn for the squirming butt. 'Daphne, this might be something or nothing… but when I followed James last night, he went to the Wallace and Simpson bank.'

'Oh. Perhaps it is the bank of one of his clients. Wait… *after closing time?*'

I nodded. 'He rang the bell, and was met by someone who looked like the manager. It seemed they knew each other. He went inside for twenty minutes, then left, and went home. It answers your initial question, but raises others.'

The frown got deeper. 'I see. But I can assure you, we have no personal connection to that bank.'

'So… any idea about a possible business connection?'

She shook her head, and stood up to leave. 'None. But in truth, Sandie, you have completed the task I gave you, and been well paid for it. Any further involvement is not required.' She held out a hand. 'Thank you so much for putting my mind at rest. I must leave now, there is much I have to do.'

I took the elegant hand, and watched her leave. Then I slumped down into my chair, and found my head shaking again. Daphne deMountford had ended our business relationship, but a little too hastily to be convincing. She'd been genuinely surprised by my additional revelations, but it was like they had triggered an automatic response.

The response to bolt, before any more awkward questions could be asked.

For someone like me, possessing the intuitive intelligence to know when someone wasn't telling me everything, it was the proverbial red rag to a bull. Yes, the easy option was there. Enjoy the large fee, shrug my shoulders, and move on.

But that wasn't me. Easy money or not, I couldn't shrug my shoulders, and simply pretend that answering one question hadn't thrown up another. The bad feeling that wasn't showing a single sign of going away was digging me in the ribs, and telling me Daphne didn't realize it, but she probably needed me more than ever... like it or not.

And that time she'd called in, she'd not smoked a single cigarette.

I closed the window again, and went back to staring at the walls.

Right then, I didn't know how, but I had to find out what it was they weren't telling me.

Both of them.

Chapter 8

The next morning, I made Archie's day by handing him a portion of the large fee from the deMountford stable. Somewhat annoyingly, he stared at the wad in his hand in disbelief.

'Um… what have I done to deserve this, boss?'

'Just… just don't look a gift-horse in the mouth. Go and buy yourself a catering-sized box of peanuts or something.'

Still he was frowning at me. 'So what have I *got to do* to deserve this then?'

'Nothing. Just call it overtime, for the time that Amazonian you have a fetish about kept you after hours.'

'I don't… ok, boss. Point taken.'

I grinned, and left him to his fantasies.

As lunchtime came I found myself trekking to the Green Mill again. Malignant grumblings were still getting bigger, and after what Tom had been interrupted from telling me the other day, I decided it might help to find out what he didn't say.

The man was oiling the bar top as I walked in. No one else seemed to be there. This time he might actually be able to complete a sentence.

He grinned as he saw me. 'As I live and breathe… Lady Sandie, the second time in a week.'

'Don't get used to it. I need your words, not… well, ok, one more of those gins wouldn't be rejected.'

He laughed, pulled out the bottle and a glass, and did as I suggested. 'You sure is a glutton for punishment. Just tip it in one of the potted plants if we get raided.'

'At this time of day?'

51

'This time of day Mr. Capone don't show, so the police know there's no one to challenge their authority.'

'Go Scarface.'

'Hey... he don't like being called that.'

'Sorry. I don't share your reverence, Tom.'

He shook his head. 'I gotta play it on the side of good business, Sandie. And right now, Mr. Capone is the good business.'

I forced my gob to shut, except to take a swig of the gin. Tom and me saw things very differently, but I guess we both had our reasons. So instead of arguing my point, I asked the question which was the purpose of coming in the first place.

'You were going to say something about the African Queen when we got interrupted the other day, Tom.'

'Geez, you still obsessing about her?'

'She is an impressive woman.'

'Hell, if I didn't know you better, I'd think you fancied her.'

'Not up my street, Tom. But I solved her problem, and found myself with another.'

'Guess you're not going to tell me, client confidentiality and all that?'

'No, I'm not going to tell you. But something got me curious, as did what you were about to say the other day before Machine Gun interrupted us.'

'Aw, gee, that was something and nothing, Sandie.'

'Try me anyway.'

He leant over closer to me, even though there was no one around to hear. 'You didn't get this from me, ok?' I nodded, my stomach playing somersaults again. 'And I can't do nothing to confirm it, but bartenders get to hear a lot of chatter, savvy?'

52

'You know anything you say is safe with me, Tom. So just get on with it, please?'

'That husband of hers, they say he's pals with the mob. Seems like it might be true as well, coz sometimes I see both of them here with the hoods.'

'Which hoods? There's a whole host of choice here in Chicago.'

'Capone's crew. I don't know nothing other than that. And I sure don't ask, if you get me?'

My stomach somersaults started to resemble a catherine-wheel on heat. 'Hell, Tom. She didn't say anything about... connections. If she had...'

'Maybe that's why she didn't. I know you would have run a mile. Did you tell her that's what you'd do?'

'Yeah, it slipped out. Maybe one or two things make sense now.'

'Hey Sandie, don't you go digging dirt and getting yourself in big trouble. Neither me or you know what you're getting into.'

I turned away, ran a hand through my long light-brown bob. 'Seems like I might have been sucked in whether I like it or not. You think Daphne knows what's going on?'

'Sandie, I said...'

'Please answer the question, Tom.'

He shrugged his shoulders. They've only been here together a couple of times. But if that James is tied into the mob, you know as well as me they keep their women out of it as much as possible. They know what's going on of course, but they don't know no details. That's as much of an answer as I can give you, Sandie. The twice they've been here, Daphne has been huddled in a booth with two of her girlfriends, giggling and drinking. Hardly said a word to her husband all night, him drinking with the crew.'

'So is that the norm these days?'

'Pretty much. The hoods in one area, their wives and girlfriends in a separate one. Then Capone and his crew can go to one of his brothels, and leave their wives to enjoy the rest of the evening without them.'

'Gee... wish I hadn't asked now.'

Tom nodded his head. 'Yeah. I see it all, but I don't see nothing, if you get me. James though, he don't do that kind of thing. When the others go, he rejoins his wife. It's kinda good to see, in these times.'

'That's something, I suppose. I'll tell you this much... Daphne thought he was being unfaithful, but it turns out he wasn't. But what he was doing raises a lot more questions.'

'You ain't gonna let it go then, against my advice?'

'I can't, Tom.' My head seemed to be shaking again, without me making it happen. 'Something odd is going on, and if it all comes out, Daphne might be caught in the aftermath.'

He pierced a stare into me. 'Do I get the feeling you care about her?'

Suddenly my head was nodding, all of its own. 'I do, for some strange reason.' I caught sight of his look. 'Hey, not in *that* way. But when we've had conversations, it seems she hasn't a clue what's going on... whatever that might be. I need to look deeper into it, but right now I don't really know how.'

He leant closer again. 'I guess no amount of polite ass-kicking from me is gonna change your mind?'

'I've got to see what's at the bottom of the well, Tom.'

'Ok then, here's a heads-up... there's a bit of a mob doo tonight. Mr. Capone and his crew are coming at eight, so it's possible your two favorite people might be here too. If you want to make sure you're here as well, you could observe them all at play, if it helps.'

'Yeah, it might. Thanks, Tom.'

'Just one thing though... you gotta be here before Capone. Once he arrives no one else is allowed in, and anyone already here can't leave until he does. Security and all that, y'know.'

'Hell. Today's Chicago, hey?'

He nodded, a little sadly. 'It ain't so bad though. The crew spend like money's going out of fashion, and anyone trapped here gets free drinks all night!'

'Sure Tom. If you close your eyes to everything else that's going on around you, that's no problem.'

'Hey Sandie... I'm a bartender, not a member of the Temperance Movement!'

Chapter 9

Walk away. Don't look back. Leave them to their lives, no matter how sordid they might be.

As I headed back to the office, every sensible warning shot my subconscious could invent was searing through my head. Every one of them missed their target. Not getting involved had gone out of the window along with the pall of fog from Daphne's chain-smoking.

I should have known better. Eight years ago when I should have walked away I couldn't, and it ended up changing my life. Maybe I'm just as stupid as those flappers I take great pleasure in deriding so much. Perhaps hindsight is a dangerous thing.

I *was* involved, whether I liked it or not. Daphne had ended our business relationship, but for some goddamn infuriating reason, I couldn't.

I could blame it on the nosy curiosity of a private investigator. Or the insane need to not leave loose ends. It could have been the caring side of my personality, which wasn't convinced by the fact Daphne apparently didn't want to know what her husband was up to, just as long as it didn't involve another woman. None of those rang true, not on their own.

There were more loose ends than a badly-frayed rope. Did she already know what I didn't? Was Tom wrong about James being involved with the mob?

Was Daphne trying to protect me, knowing I had an aversion to gangsters?

And just what the hell was James up to anyway?

Walk away? That wasn't an option, not with all the intriguing rope ends flailing my sensible side into painful submission.

As I headed up the stairs to the office, I'd already made the fatal decision.

Archie gave me another curious look as I gifted him the rest of the afternoon off, and told him to go buy his catering-size box of peanuts. He opened his mouth to say something, but then clearly thought better of it, grabbed his jacket, and disappeared gratefully.

He likely thought I was buttering him up, so I could ask him to do something dangerous in the very near future.

I didn't tell him the only dangerous things flying around were the thoughts in my head.

I locked the office door, went upstairs and stretched out onto the couch in my apartment. There were a few hours to kill until it was time to head to the Green Mill, but I didn't want Archie or the telephone to disturb the battle I was raging with myself.

After an hour wrestling with non-existent gremlins, I made myself a promise. Ok, maybe a compromise. I would go to the Mill that evening, just to observe. If what I saw led me to believe James was seriously involved with the mob, then it really would be time to walk away.

Somehow I would have to, before I got seriously involved too.

I chose my outfit... not that there was much choice. Too old to do the flapper thing and dress to get noticed, and too sensible not to get drawn into that craziness anyway, most of the clothes I possessed were designed to do the opposite. *Not* being noticed was a far better option in my line of work.

I chose a dark red dress with a hemline just below the knee... still a little risqué, but nowhere near as revealing as the dresses the flappers wore. I pulled out a simple burgundy cloche hat... no bow or silly feathers. It all looked a little on the frumpy side, but I would be on my own, and the last thing I wanted was for some opportunistic guy, hood or otherwise, to approach me while I was staking out the action.

I did succumb to a string of fake pearls; something to take eyes away from the fact the neckline was a little too low for my comfort.

I gave myself a spin in front of the bedroom mirror. I would do... smart enough to convince folks I was there for an evening out, but frumpy enough to avoid being the belle of the ball.

Now all I had to do was wait... and not work myself into ever-decreasing circles of possible scenarios.

That was just as hard as actually going to the Green Mill whilst Capone was there.

A light, freezing rain was beginning to fall as I closed the sidewalk door, and headed quickly to the corner of North Broadway and Lawrence. I'd thrown a light-grey coat around my shoulders, but the cold Chicago night still made me shiver, even on the short walk to the bar.

Maybe it wasn't the cold.

As I turned the corner, the queue for the Uptown Theatre was already stretching almost as far as the Mill's doorway. People were beginning to file into the Atrium, the theatre doors having just opened. It was Friday night, so most of the city's entertainment joints would be filling up in the next hour.

It was approaching seven-thirty. I hoped I'd timed my arrival well... late enough not to be the first there, but early enough so I could choose the best booth to see what I needed to see.

Tom greeted me with a slightly knowing frown, a little surprised I'd actually turned up. He pointed out Capone's favourite booth, and where the womenfolk would likely sit. Then he glanced around to make sure no one was watching, and quickly poured me a couple of shots of the real stuff. Then he nodded silently to the booth he'd clearly earmarked for me, and the potted plant right next to it.

I nodded to say I'd understood, and took up my position.

It looked like I'd timed it pretty well. There were a few punters in the place, mostly in couples. Three guys were sitting together a few booths along from mine. I'd got a spot opposite the top end of the bar, far enough into the room to be able to see what went on without being too conspicuous. The jazz band was already playing away, rattling off a few laid-back numbers while they waited for the main crowd to arrive.

They knew which celebrity was heading their way of course, and that they had to be nicely warmed up before he arrived. Displeasing him with some bum notes wouldn't do at all.

I got Tom to refill my shot glasses, but took it easy... getting merry wouldn't help my task that evening. I fell back into position again, and another half-hour passed, which allowed my personal butterflies to warm up along with the band. Yet again I found myself questioning why I was even there at all, and this time the doubts seemed to be far more voracious than the reasons.

I'd almost decided to give into them, say a goodnight to Tom, and actually walk away. Then the main door burst open, and I realized I was a minute too late making my final decision.

Two hoods breezed in, their weapons brandished for all to see, and took a quick look around. One of them disappeared again, and a minute later he was back. But this time, he wasn't alone.

Far from it. Suddenly the bar seemed full of people, as what felt like a rush of noisy men and women flocked through the door.

I guess there weren't really that many of them, but after the relative tranquility of the early evening, in the space of ten seconds the new arrivals made sure it would be peaceful no more.

Mr. Capone had arrived.

Chapter 10

The city's favourite gangster breezed in, together with a flock of significant others. Three of them had machine guns, which they used to great effect to make sure those inside knew their boss was in the building, and he should therefore command respect.

Two other men looked almost as well-attired, and likely just as well-versed, and took up their positions in the favoured booth. My heart sank.

One of them was James deMountford.

Daphne was there too, in the company of three other women. They headed to the booth Tom had said they likely would, and the bartender took them all a tray of drinks. My ex-client didn't even notice I was there, too wrapped up laughing and giggling with her girlfriends.

I was kind of glad she was oblivious to my presence.

It was a pretty fair bet two other hoods were stationed outside, stopping anyone else from entering. Until Capone decided to leave I was trapped inside, along with everyone else. That I didn't mind. But what I did mind was that James was looking a lot more comfortable than I felt comfortable with.

Daphne had pulled one over on me, desperate to know if her husband was being unfaithful, and already knowing I would have refused the job if I'd been told who it was they both hung around with.

I watched her and James, feeling like I'd been well and truly railroaded, but still obsessively curious about what James was doing at a bank he seemed to have no connection with... after hours. It was looking like in some shape or form he worked for Capone's organization, and although I had a personal aversion to the mob, I'd known for some time that Johnny Torrio, the gangster who'd brought Scarface to Chicago, didn't bank his legitimate businesses at Wallace and Simpson.

My father discovered that fact, just before he died.

Maybe Capone did bank there, but it wasn't likely. Even if he did, there was no sensible reason James would be visiting the place after hours, unless he was up to something seriously criminal.

For the curiosity of a private detective, it was all very puzzling.

Too puzzling for my own health.

Tom shook me out of my confusion, dropping a couple of shots on my table, and smiling a little pensively. 'Compliments of Mr. Capone,' he said, knowing I already knew where they'd come from. I'd idly watched Tom and his junior bartender serving up drinks to the other people imprisoned in the bar… who didn't look that bothered they weren't able to leave.

An hour passed. The band was hyping it up, much to Capone's delight. He and his henchmen seemed to be enjoying themselves. James was too, looking for all the world like he was where he belonged.

I cringed inside, and then cringed again as Daphne and one of her girlfriends found a little space, and gave it large as they gyrated away to the music, much to the male punter's delight. The drinks were flowing constantly, and I noticed the friend making sure Daphne didn't hold back on her alcoholic consumption.

I watched, fascinated, as she pulled her moves on the floor. In truth it was hard not to. A trained dancer, all legs and arms, she didn't need to be that good to be *good*. The sexy sass and her formidable natural assets made it hard for anyone to wrench their eyes away, and the fact she was dressed to impress made it all the more of a not-to-be-missed show.

I didn't know her very well, but as the band rattled off their numbers, she seemed to have unlimited energy, and a limitless capacity for alcohol. The girl she was dancing with seemed to be paying her a lot of attention, and she was getting it reciprocated, much to the approval of Capone and his cronies.

I had an uninterrupted view of the floor show, but what I was seeing didn't exactly please me. Daphne was making all the right moves, but while everyone else had huge grins on their faces, she didn't. The girl she was dancing with, a pretty girl with blonde curls who looked a few years younger, dressed in a split-seam flapper dress, and a feathered headband that enveloped her curls, was making sure their bodies were a bit closer together than was considered decent.

She looked like I imagined the fictitious Roxie Hart would look. That didn't bode well for my unsettled status either, knowing the true story behind the play.

Then, their lips met in a passionate kiss. They both looked to be well on their way to being drunk, but somehow that didn't explain the intensity of the kiss, or the look they gave each other when their lips eventually parted.

Daphne turned away, and then staggered a little. Still she wasn't exactly smiling, but she had clearly reached her alcoholic limit. James hadn't noticed, locked in a deep conversation with his boss. But the girl on the other end of Daphne's lips had. She wrapped a concerned arm around her waist, and said something I couldn't hear as her other hand caressed her cheek.

63

Daphne nodded, and despite the fact it was impossible for a black woman, she seemed to look a little green as they headed past me, and through the open doorway next to the rear end of the bar, no doubt heading for the washrooms to try and sober up.

I shook my head, starting to wonder if Daphne had turned the story she gave me on its head. Maybe it was *her* having the affair… with another woman? On the flip side of the coin, if that was the case, why was she clearly so cut up about James's possible infidelity?

Yet another illogical fact that didn't make sense.

I went back to my free drink, wondering what the hell I'd got myself into. The distasteful tang on my lips, and the sudden realization in my head, was telling me it would be wise to get myself out of the murk as soon as I could leg it without upsetting anyone with a gun.

Someone breezed past me on his way to the washrooms; it looked like one of the three guys who were sitting together before Capone arrived. Such was my new-found misery, I was too preoccupied beating myself up for my insane stupidity to take much notice.

Then Tom answered the phone behind the bar, and went over to James, who stood up, and followed him to the bar. Tom slapped the phone onto the bar top next to James, and he picked up the receiver. Just ten feet away from me as he answered the call that must have been for him, I was glad he hadn't a clue who I was. Explaining why I was yet again watching what he was up to would have been nigh on impossible, when I couldn't even explain it to myself.

At least, not without convincing my sensible self I actually was insane.

Things were turning out just like they would in any bar before the days of prohibition. The jazz band was living it larger than ever, the punters were enjoying the free drinks and the foot-tapping music, and the place was a hive of fun and jollity. Yet if I could have, I was ready to go home, leave them all to their frivolity, and drown my sorrows in a quiet whisky.

Then something happened to change all that.

You know how you do… decide you need one more drink, and glance ahead to the bar as you get to your feet. I did exactly that; and saw James as he put down the phone. Just as he began to turn away again, he saw something that brought a lovely smile to his face.

It happened so fast… in the split second I saw the smile, my head told me Daphne must have just appeared through the doorway from the foyer. But I didn't even have time to glance to see if it was her, until it was too late.

Three shots rang out, one after the other in quick succession. As all three slugs hit James in the chest, he crashed to the floor, the smile turning to an anguished crease of horrified realization. For a few seconds, my instinct made me run to him, even though I knew he was a moment away from dying. It was only as I reached him I turned to what he'd seen in the moment before his death.

It *was* Daphne. She was standing just inside the doorway, a shocked, disbelieving expression on her face.

Her right arm hung listlessly down by her side. In her hand was a chrome-plated Luger.

Chapter 11

It was like the world turned to silent, slow motion. The music stuttered to a stop, the people around the bar stared in disbelief.

Even in Chicago, what had happened was enough to stun everyone.

Daphne let out a strangled kind of scream. The gun in her hand crashed to the floor. Shaking hands flew to her face, and then her legs gave way. She fell to her knees, her big eyes still full of disbelief at what she'd somehow done.

And then all around me was a flurry of movement. Capone and his men were the first to react, flying to their feet and heading for the second door, no doubt on their way to the tunnel that led to the far side of the street.

No doubt thinking they might be next.

Most of the other punters didn't want to know either. With Capone beating a hasty retreat, they weren't going to wait around for awkward questions to be asked by the police Tom was already calling.

In what seemed like seconds the room was virtually empty. There wasn't much space between the desolate Daphne and the exit door, but somehow the drinkers managed to empty their glasses and find their way out.

The girlfriend had her arm around Daphne, whispering something in her ear. The junior bartender started running around the room, making sure any signs of illegal alcohol were removed. Tom had put the phone down, and was kneeling beside James, feeling his neck.

'He's dead,' he said flatly.

I dropped down beside him, and saw the desperate look in his eyes as he shook his head. A seemingly-decent man had lost his life in his bar, shot dead by his wife, for no apparent reason. Apart from the tragic loss, his mind was already thinking ahead to the sobering fact his business was sure to suffer.

I turned to Daphne, and the curly blonde doing her best to give her comfort. Tears were streaming down her face, and her wretched sobs were the only sounds in the room. Then without warning, she shook herself free of her girlfriend's arm, and tried to crawl across the floor to her husband on her hands and knees.

Tom and another man stopped her. 'I think you've done enough, don't you, Daphne?' he snarled.

'Leave me alone...' she screamed.

They weren't going to leave her alone. Between them they wrenched her to her feet. She tried to lash out, but it did nothing other than make her inebriated state a whole lot more obvious. If Tom hadn't got her long arms pinned behind her back, she would have crashed to the floor.

'No...' she cried out.

The other man had found a length of rope, and was busy tying her hands. 'Bit late for regrets, isn't it?' he growled.

I couldn't stay anonymous anymore. I stood next to her, and looked her in her tear-stained face. 'What did you do, Daphne?' I said quietly, and as calmly as I could.

For a moment she stared blankly at me, trying to work out who it was asking the question. Then her eyes filled with fresh tears, and she turned her eyes away. *'I... I can't...'*

The sound of police bells jangled their way to a screeching stop outside. The guy who had a firm grip on the perpetrator whipped her away from me, and shoved her into a seat in the booth next to the door. *'Don't you dare move...'* he warned her.

He didn't really have to worry. So consumed by grief and alcohol, Daphne deMountford wasn't capable of going anywhere.

Frank Kowalski sat down in the booth opposite me. We'd known each other as long as I could remember; well before my father died, and all through the eight years I'd run the business since. He was one of the increasingly-rare good guys in the Chicago police department... incorruptible, and pretty much as honest as any good guy was these days. A few years older than me, he was my father's go-to guy in the police, and so naturally he became mine too.

Over the years I'd become a thorn in his side, according to him, but whenever he told me that, it was always with a wry smile on his face. We kind of had a soft spot for each other, and when the opportunity arose, scratched each other's backs by sharing information... and a drink or two.

If it hadn't been for him, I would likely have caved in years ago.

He fixed his time-honoured stare into me. 'So what happened here, Sandie? And what the hell were you doing here anyway, after you told me you'd never set foot in the place again?'

'Can I answer one question at a time, Frank?'

He shook his head, like he'd been expecting the retort. 'Sure.'

'It seems a drunk Daphne deMountford went to the washroom, and then came back and pumped three slugs into her husband.'

He frowned. '*Seems?* It looks pretty cut and dried to me. And there must have been a list of witnesses as long as my arm, if most of them hadn't disappeared into the night.'

It was my turn to shake my head. 'Yes Frank… it *seems* that was what happened.'

'You telling me some phantom apparition pulled the trigger?'

'No, but to answer your second question, Daphne deMountford was a client of mine.'

'Geez… you remember what I said about a th…'

'Yeah, sure. A thorn in your side. But this particular rose is struggling to believe what actually happened.'

'You wanna tell me why?'

I told him why. All about me vindicating her husband, and my business relationship with Daphne being concluded by her. I did omit to tell him just where James had actually gone when I'd followed him. Right then, that wasn't for his ears.

He looked at me with raised eyebrows. 'So the dead guy wasn't being unfaithful, but she shot him anyway?'

'Apparently.'

'So what is this, Sandie? You think there's more to it?'

'Can't say, Frank. Not right now.'

'Now you're filling me with dread.'

'Relax, my friend. I was looking at James when the shots were fired. I didn't see who pulled the trigger, so I can't really tell you anything.'

'Except there was only one person with a gun in her hand.'

'Exactly.'

'Still filling me with dread, Sandie.'

I got to my feet, my body telling me that cozying up under the bed sheets was where it needed to be. Apart from Frank's deputy, sitting interviewing Tom in another booth, we were the last ones there. Daphne had been carted off to the cells almost as soon as the police arrived, and everyone else seemed to have slipped away unnoticed.

'How about I come and see you in the morning, Frank? It's past the time all good children should be in bed, and a night's sleep might help me remember something my head can't latch onto right now.'

He let out a deep sigh, and then nodded. 'Sure thing, Sandie. Can't see this is gonna take much wrapping up, but it's always nice to see you. Call me before you turn up, ok?'

I left him closing his notebook without writing a single word in it, said a sympathetic goodnight to Tom, and headed out into the freezing November air. I shivered again, but this time knew for sure it wasn't just the temperature.

The evening I'd almost chickened out on had turned into one I would never forget. For all the wrong reasons. For reasons that as of right then, remained a mystery. Not a good scenario for an inquisitive private investigator.

On the surface, Frank was right. Murders don't get any more cut and dried. But despite the nasty taste in my mouth, that even the finest whisky wouldn't have a hope in hell of taking away, there was a little voice grumbling away in the back of my mind.

A faint niggling doubt, telling me not everything was as wrapped up as Frank would like it to be.

Chapter 12

The whisky didn't take away the nasty taste, even though I'd downed a larger one than usual. It didn't seem to help the little voice in my head fall into an inebriated sleep either.

Something didn't make sense. Actually, more than a something didn't make sense.

On the surface, Daphne and James had a relationship made in heaven. I'd already vindicated him of infidelity, so what possible motive could she have had for killing him? Then again, she'd omitted to tell me a few salient facts, like he was involved with the mob. Had she also left out a few other *very* salient facts I should have been told?

Even if she had, why pump three slugs into him in a bar full of people, where a multitude of witnesses saw her do it? The two of them must have spent a fair proportion of their lives when it would have been far easier to do away with him with no witnesses anywhere near.

Maybe the Temperance movement had it right after all... the evils of alcohol were the demons that stalked America.

Somehow I couldn't wrap my head around drink being the sole reason why a woman who seemingly had it all would suddenly and unexplainably rip it all away. Because she definitely had... she and I both knew that without James she was nothing.

Somewhere on the railroad track, there was a junction I didn't know existed.

I crawled out of bed a little later the next morning. Sleep had been a while coming, and so was waking, turning me into more of a rag doll than usual. I dressed without really knowing what I was doing, and wandered down to the office to find Archie already there.

He didn't seem too happy when I told him the subject of his fantasies had murdered her husband.

'Aw hell... why did she pump slugs into him? From what I've seen of her, she could have snapped his neck like a twig.'

'You been reading too many comic books again, Archie?'

'No... but...'

'Put your imagination away. I'm going to the station in an hour, to see if Frank and me can piece anything together.'

'But... it sounds open and shut.'

'Yeah, I know.'

'You don't sound convinced, Sandie. Please, say you're not convinced?'

'I'm not, but I still can't see there's any way your favourite client couldn't have done it. I'm more concerned about the why.'

He pulled out a packet of peanuts. 'Guess I'd better drown my sorrows then, while you find out *why* she did it.'

'Don't look so despondent. I'm sure she'll appreciate the occasional visit from you at Cook County.'

'Ok, ok. Just... it's not funny, please remember that. Murder is never funny.'

'Sorry, Archie. Just my defence mechanism. You know as well as me it kicks in when something doesn't feel right.'

'I forgive you, boss.'

Two hours later, I sat down on the other side of Frank's desk. He didn't exactly look full of the joys of spring either.

'Not the best of days, hey Frank?'

72

He shook his head like I didn't really need to ask. 'Sometimes things are far easier with a simple mob killing, Sandie.'

I was about to say it kind of was a mob killing, but shut my gob just in time. 'So what's the score, now the light of day shines brightly on a dark deed?'

He looked like he didn't want to tell me, but then seemed to decide he had to. 'Daphne deMountford will be charged shortly, and then transferred to Cook County jail to await trial.'

'Oh come on, Frank. She won't last a week in that hellhole.'

'Ain't my concern. None of it is anymore.'

'What are you saying?' I asked, narrowing my eyes at his words, and the speed things seemed to be moving.

'Look Sandie... I don't have point on this anymore. What goes down is out of my control.'

'So who does?'

'Dabney.'

'What, that sniveling creep? Isn't he in Dever's back pocket?'

'For sure. And our esteemed mayor wants this tied up tighter than a Thanksgiving turkey. It ain't doing his chances of re-election any good.'

'So it's all done and dusted then, without even an investigation?'

He threw me a narrow-eyed stare, like I'd said the wrong thing. 'Let's be fair, murders in this city don't get much more cut-and-dried, do they?'

'On the surface, no. Not when nobody cares.'

He threw me a thin file, and then stood and walked to the window. 'You know me better than that, Sandie. But do you want me to get thrown on the scrapheap, by going against Dabney and the Mayor? I ain't exactly a spring chicken. That'll be me sweeping the streets.'

I found myself short of words, comforting or otherwise. So instead I opened the file. It was a forensics report on the gun in Daphne's hand. It didn't make good reading, even if it wasn't exactly a surprise.

'It *was* the gun that fired the slugs then.'

Frank turned back to me. 'I take it from that you kinda wanted it not to be?'

'I... I don't know. I've gone over the night in my mind a hundred times, but I still can't work out *why* she would do it... and do it at the Green Mill of all places.'

He nodded, in a resigned kind of way. 'Me either. But it don't make no difference now. She's guilty, and there ain't a goddamn thing either of us can do about it.'

'Maybe not.'

My two words made his hands fly into the air. 'Sandie... you got a thing about her, or what?'

'No, I haven't. But unlike the mayor and everyone else below him, I don't want to think she's going to be sent to the gallows just because it's convenient for the city.'

He slumped back into his well-worn chair, and lit another cigar. 'Guess I should have known you'd take that attitude. You're a pain in my...'

'Yeah, I know. And I also know there's nothing you can do without being sideswiped into early retirement.'

He must have seen the look in my eyes, one he knew well. 'But..?'

'But *I* don't have that noose hanging over me.'

'Sandie...'

'Look, Frank. I'm not saying she didn't do it. But until I know *why* she did it, I can't put it to bed. Not my bed anyway.'

'Should've known.'

'I think you did know, deep down. And I also think you need to know why she did it too. So let me go see her, try and find out a bit more from the horse's mouth.'

'I ain't supposed to allow... aw, geez.'

Chapter 13

Frank walked me to the holding cells, but when I got there the desk sergeant said Daphne already had a visitor. We both frowned, until he explained.

'Her lawyer turned up a short while ago. She don't look much like a lawyer to me, but she shoved a business card in my face so I had to let her in. I said they'd have to talk through the bars though, and now her time is almost up.'

Something told me I knew who was visiting, and if that something was correct, she sure wasn't a member of the legal profession. 'Pretty young thing; blonde curls?'

'Yeah, sounds like her.'

I glanced to Frank, shook my head. 'I think your sergeant here has been taken for a ride, if it's who I think it is.'

He looked at me curiously. At the Green Mill, Daphne's girlfriend had disappeared just after most everyone else after Tom had called the police, so Frank hadn't set eyes on her. But I surely had.

So much for love and loyalty.

Frank made for the door to the cell block corridor, so I followed. He glanced back, the frown still on his brow. 'You know that broad then?'

'I don't *know* her, but I spent two hours watching her cavort around the floor with the accused.'

'So she might be a lawyer?'

'Unlikely. But I suppose...'

As the door to the walkway clunked aside, it was more than clear that, lawyer or not, there was more to their relationship than just business. Their lips parted hastily, a stolen kiss through the bars of the cell. Their hands separated hastily as they saw us. Blondie gathered herself together, and growled out the words at me in a very lawyer-like fashion. 'Who the hell are you?'

Frank didn't seem to like the attitude. 'She's a concerned citizen, and I'm the one in charge... and your time is up. I suggest you leave my precinct, before I charge you with trespass.'

'My client and I haven't concluded our business.'

'From what I saw, it's more like funny business you ain't concluded. Ten seconds, then I lock you up too.'

'You have no right, you... bully.' She flustered out a protest, but then decided she'd been well and truly rumbled, so hastily grabbed her bag, gave Daphne a silly wave and a dark look, and trotted away. *'I'll be back...'* she couldn't help hissing as a parting shot. I wasn't sure who it was aimed at.

I put my hand on Frank's arm, and gave him as coy a glance as I could manage. 'I might get further if it's just the two of us,' I hinted quietly.

He almost looked relieved. 'Sure, Sandie. Just call the sergeant when you're done. Best I'm not here anyway.'

He walked away, let himself out of the walkway exit, and disappeared, no doubt breathing a huge sigh of relief. I turned and walked over to Daphne. It was the first time I'd seen her up close and personal since the previous night, and what I saw wasn't so easy to look at.

The elegant confidence was gone. The neat black bob was neat no more, her lank hair streaked with sweat and tears. Her big brown eyes were red and swollen, and lines of hours-old mascara diluted by tears were drawn down her cheeks.

A shaky hand clutched one of the bars like she needed to hold herself up, and the once-sexy dress looked like she'd slept in it for a week.

All of a sudden, far from looking younger than she actually was, she seemed a hell of a lot older.

And despite what she'd done, my heart went out to her. She'd lost the husband she loved... or had once loved.

I fumbled in my bag, and held out a handkerchief. 'Clean your face. It's not a good look.' I tried to soften my voice, but wasn't sure I'd managed it. She took the square of cloth anyway, and wiped her cheeks without a word. The silence didn't last long.

'What are you doing here? Come to gloat?' she hissed, in a voice that sounded like someone else's.

'Sure, honey. I get off on seeing a client who overpays me banged up like a wild animal.'

I saw her eyes fill with tears. She let out a little sob, dabbed her eyes like it was painful to touch them. It probably was. 'I'm sorry. I don't know what's happening to me...'

Furtive eyes flicked around, giving away the fact she was scared to death. A caged animal maybe wasn't that far from the truth. But I couldn't lie to her. 'I have a working relationship with Frank, the detective who came in with me. They're going to charge you with murder, Daphne.'

She let out a louder sob, turned away and covered her face with her hands. *'I... I don't...'*

'Daphne, you can't put three rounds into someone in a bar and hope to get away with it. I want to do what I can to help, but...'

She turned back to me. 'I was drunk... off my face if you must know. I don't remember...'

Her words were slurred, mostly by the high emotion flying around, and partly from the excessive alcohol she was still sobering up from. She seemed like her mind and her body were on separate planets, as she struggled to pull reality together, and accept what was happening to her. I groaned to myself… it appeared to be down to me to give her the pertinent facts, even though I really didn't want to.

'Forensics found the gun in your hand was the one that killed James, Daphne.'

She cried out her anguish, but the words that followed were almost whispered. *'I don't understand. I didn't… I didn't have a gun.'*

'Daphne, I was there. I saw the slugs hit James, and then I looked around at you. The Luger was in your hand, before you dropped it to the floor.'

'A… a Luger? I have a Luger, back at the house. James insisted I have it, for protection. But I never take it out with me. I hate guns…'

'Was it a chrome-plated Luger?'

She nodded slowly, realizing the only way I would know to ask that was if I'd seen it at the Green Mill.

'It's not looking good, you have to understand. And Dever wants it wrapped up like yesterday, so that isn't helping either. I don't know what I can do.'

She slumped down onto the only just less than hard bench. 'Nancy said she could get me off, if…'

'Nancy? I take it that's Blondie, your girlfriend?'

'Don't look at me like that. She came on to me a few weeks ago, and… and I sort of liked it. Then one night we got drunk, and… well, you know.'

'Sure, I know. Going on what I saw last night, she's expert in getting you over your limit. *So why, Daphne?*'

'Look, it doesn't count with another woman, right?'

'If you want to see it that way.'

'Ok, so I wasn't that keen. Saw it as a bit of sexy fun. I think she viewed it different. But after what she just said…'

'What she said?'

Daphne stood up, and shuffled like a broken woman over to the bars, on legs that didn't seem like they wanted to work properly. 'Sandie, my head is still spinning. She wasn't making any sense, going on about some kind of key.'

'Key? A key to what?'

She started to shake her head, but then thought better of it, and put a hand to it instead. 'No idea. I don't know anything about a key. The police took my house keys off me, but they're the only keys I have. Then you turned up, and Nancy was gone. I don't understand...'

Her desolate fingers wrapped around the bar again. My hand seemed to have a mind of its own, and curled around hers to try and let her know I cared. 'I don't understand either. What the hell would Nancy want with some kind of key?'

'She said if I gave her the key, she knew people who would get me off. But I don't remember anything of last night, Sandie.'

I nodded my head, as one or two pieces of the jigsaw began to slot into place. Trouble was, I still didn't know if they were in the right place. 'Sounds like Nancy only really wanted one thing from you, Daphne.'

Her head lowered. 'I thought she was a special friend. She's a dancer, like me, but unlike me she's got a long-term job in the troupe at the Chicago Theatre. Kindred spirits, you might say. But now I'm wondering if it was all some kind of play.'

I couldn't help smiling. 'Yeah... she looks like I imagine Roxie Hart would look.'

Daphne didn't seem amused, and I realized it likely wasn't the best thing to say. Then she made everything worse.

'I'm all alone now, Sandie. I have no one.'

I said it. Maybe it was something else I shouldn't have said, but I just couldn't stop the words tumbling out.

'You're not alone. You have me.'

Chapter 14

I left Daphne looking like her world had imploded around her. She had every reason... it had imploded. Her tearful last words were reverberating around my brain, mostly because they were gut-wrenchingly true.

The friends that were really James's friends had deserted her, and the one special friend she thought she had turned out to only want one thing, which wasn't her. For sure, other than me, she had no one.

Maybe wrapping my hand around hers was giving her the wrong impression, but I didn't think so. Guilty or not, the poor girl needed someone to stand beside her, and from what I was seeing, little ole me was the only one who would.

Frank still had a bit of fighting spirit in him, but he was worn down by what the city had become, and what it expected of him in cases like these. His overriding but depressing situation was that he was a few years from retirement, and had to toe the city line if he wanted his pension.

I was the only lifeline Daphne had, and the only way Frank could unearth whatever truth was out there, without being seen to do so.

No pressure then.

On my way out of the cell block, I smiled as sweetly as I could manage at the sergeant. 'That fake business card... you thrown it in the bin yet?'

He shook his head, picked it up from the desk and clicked his lips as he looked at it. 'I knew it was fake, but it ain't my job to check visitor's identities, just what they bring in that they shouldn't. Way above my pay grade to start making phone calls.'

I kept the smile. If he had phoned the number on the card, Nancy would have never got to see Daphne, and neither of us would be any the wiser about what she really wanted. 'It's not an issue. But I guess that card is full of crap. It's no use to you, so would you mind letting me have it?'

He handed it over. 'As you say, it's no use to us. Do your worst.'

I looked at the card as I left the station, shaking my head with a vague kind of unamused amusement. *'Nancy Pelowski, attorney to the well-heeled,'* sounded every bit as fake as she was.

But *who* was she? Obviously she had an agenda that didn't include a penchant for girl-on-girl action. I couldn't discount the possibility that it had all been an elongated sting, which had worked its way towards the devastating night at the Green Mill.

Why?

It had to be something to do with the mysterious key. Nancy had wasted no time in turning up at Daphne's cell, and making sure she knew the nightmare would end if she told her where the key was.

Daphne had no idea what Nancy was referring to. That I believed. Given the desolate state of her, telling me more lies wasn't in her crumpled deck of cards.

But why was Nancy so sure she would know about the key?

And was Nancy even her real name?

There was one way to know for sure. I needed to scour the city to find her, and persuade her to tell me. But if what she'd told Daphne about her profession was true, there was one possible starting point.

On the rare occasions I felt the need for a little vaudeville nonsense, I spent the evening at the Chicago Theatre. The friendly elderly guy who was imprisoned during the day in the ticket booth on the sidewalk outside, also worked backstage in the evenings. I'd done a little job for him a year ago, uncovering the truth behind the floozy his son had planned to marry... until I revealed her true intentions.

He'd be sympathetic to my problems. And he knew everything there was to know about the shows, and the people who performed in them.

His craggy face lit up as he saw me. A true Chicagoan who was born at the end of the civil war, the loyalties of his parents had always been questionable, but his loyalty to his city had never been. He was as depressed as me at what Chicago was reverting to. I knew he would tell me everything he could to help a good cause... and that was likely to be an awful lot.

'Hey, Wyatt... how's ticket-booth prison?'

He laughed, and gave me his infectious smile. 'Aw, y'know Sandie... watching what them passing folks get up to, and hearing what they say, is never boring.'

'I guess a cell with a view is heaven on Earth for someone who watches people like you, huh?'

'Got that right. So what brings you to my hatch after nine months... a ticket for tonight, or information?' he grinned.

'Wow... you remember how long... has it *really* been that long?' I smiled incredulously.

'Sure thing. I always said you were my favourite customer.'

'Which you say to every single woman.'

'Aw geez, you got me sussed,' he said as he shook his head, knowing full well I would.

'How's that son of yours doing?'

'Good. Got hisself a new girl now… a nice little broad this time.'

'That's a good outcome then.'

'Thanks to you and your terrier mentality.'

'You say the nicest things, Wyatt,' I grinned, leaning an arm on the ledge of the open hatch. 'But now this terrier is biting at heels again.'

'Might have known you didn't come for the scintillating conversation,' he said as he narrowed his eyes.

'Don't do yourself down. I'm always drawn to your booth on the rare occasions I pass by. But, yes, I am craving your invaluable insights.'

'Anything I can do, Sandie.'

'I'm looking into a girl who dances here. Goes by the name of Nancy.'

He nodded his head. 'Yeah, she's one of the troupe. Ain't no surprise you're on her case.'

My eyebrows raised. Partly because her name really was Nancy, and partly by what Wyatt said. 'She got a reputation?'

He leaned closer to me, spoke in low tones. 'Nah.'

'Um… then why did you say that, bud?'

He pointed two fingers at his eyes. 'She got black eyes, see? They's furtive, untrustworthy. Like I seen with that tramp my son took up with. Wouldn't trust that Nancy as far as I could throw her, which at my age ain't nowhere at all.'

'Hmm… I'll take you word for it… literally. I need a word with her. She working tonight?'

85

He looked at me like I should know. 'Them gals, they work six nights a week, Sandie. Sure, she'll be here. But you ain't gonna get anything out of her with fifty others around. Take my advice, meet her at the stage door after the show.'

'What time does it finish?

'Ten-ish. Depends how many hecklers get frisky. Can never be sure to within fifteen minutes or so. Best you buy a ticket, then you'll know.'

'Always the salesman, hey Wyatt?'

'Get me a commission on each one, Sandie.'

I bought two tickets. I'd been railroaded, but in the nicest possible way. It would have been easy enough to wait around at the stage door for the show to finish, but it was likely to be below freezing, so spending the time in the warm of the auditorium sounded like a better idea.

And through a pair of theatre binoculars, I might even be able to watch the furtive black eyes Wyatt was so keen to point out.

Chapter 15

I took Archie with me that evening. Partly because a woman alone in a theatre was a little unusual, and partly because I needed some moral support.

He looked a little overawed at the impressive neoclassical architecture, modeled on the Arc de Triomphe in Paris. The sheer size and grandeur of the place was a little overawing too... but as we took our seats in the upper circle, chosen so I could slip away just before the end without it being too obvious, for once he didn't seem to have much to say.

I'd brought him up to speed, told him why we were there, and that he'd have to make his own way home afterwards. Then the massive Wurlitzer thundered out an ear splitting number to make sure everyone knew the show was starting, the lights dimmed, and the floor show kicked off. All four of our eyes were instantly seeking out the object of our desires.

Blondie was there, doing her stuff with seven others. I saw a grin spread over Archie's face. Then he seemed to pull himself together, and focused his binoculars where they needed to be, not on the bits that were admittedly more appealing.

'Those eyes sure are shifty,' he muttered.

'How can you tell that? All she's doing is cavorting her stuff.'

'Dunno. Maybe because she's just going through the motions, not exactly getting into the spirit.'

He was right. As I watched her making her moves, it was like watching a bad actress in a bad movie. A very attractive actress with everything in the right place for sure... but she'd never make the big time. Maurine Watkins' play of the same name as the theatre thundered into my mind.

I'd already thought she looked like I imagined Roxie Hart would look. From what I'd read of the play's plot, watching her emotionless performance , the similarities were quickly becoming more remarkable.

I had to admit the show was excellent. It was close to ten, and there hadn't been any interruptions from over-enthusiastic guys. The dance troupe had come onto stage for the final extravaganza. I looked at Archie, telling him silently it was time for me to leave. He nodded to me, and then went back to ogling the eight beauties taking all his attention away from the jazz singer belting his heart out.

I slipped away, strolled back through the multi-storey atrium that was almost deserted, and out through the main entrance. Then I turned to the right, and along the side of the huge half-block-sized building. Wyatt had told me how to reach the stage door, and not be seen doing it. At the back of the theatre, the door was situated halfway along. The right side of the alley was lit by lamps, and led to the street where those giving the performers a lift home parked their cars. The left, narrower part of the alley was shared with the adjoining Chinese restaurant, and was in darkness.

If I was to stand any chance of confronting the delectable Nancy, that was where I had to wait.

Wyatt didn't know if she was usually picked up by anyone, or if she made her own way home. I had no choice but to take the chance, and hope it was the latter.

My heart sank as I rounded the corner to the rear of the theatre. Up ahead I could see the bright light bulbs framing the stage door sign, and the glow of the low-powered lamps lighting up the far side of the wide part of the alley. But where I was seemed like the light had never penetrated it since time began. In the gloom I could make out a litter-strewn, damp, open corridor, punctuated by three wooden refuse crates... and likely a few hundred rats.

And quite possibly a drunk or two, although I couldn't see any right then. I could see two men, waiting by the stage door. One looked just like I would expect the boyfriend of a troupe dancer to look, one looked well dressed and self-assured.

He was clearly a hood.

I couldn't see anyone else. I slunk up closer to the stage door. I likely still had a few minutes to wait...the girls would have to change before they left, but it was a safe bet the show had only just finished. And stage performers who worked evenings didn't exactly hang about chatting at the end of a show.

I'd reached the shelter of the last industrial waste bin. Just twenty feet from the stage door, if I concealed myself behind it I could see when Nancy appeared, and hopefully follow her to wherever she lived, putting the fear of god into her somewhere en route. There was a chance one of the guys outside the door was waiting for her, but that was one I would just have to take.

I looked around. Crouching down behind the waste bin was hardly going to delight me, but I didn't want one of the men to spot me and ruin my evening. I glanced to the moonless dark sky, asking myself why I did what I did... but then was glad I had crouched down.

As my eyes fell back to the filthy ground, I spotted someone walk around the corner of the dark side of the alley, and start heading towards the stage door.

I was surrounded by men. Most likely their only intentions were innocent, but that wasn't really the point. A woman lurking in a back alley in Chicago just wasn't done, and there would inevitably be questions.

I couldn't simply join the other waiting men. Nancy would spot me instantly, and definitely bolt. It was a raging certainty she could run twice as fast as me. The other guy walking through the dark alley would see me for sure, if I didn't take some kind of cover.

Cover? What cover?

Oh no. Please don't tell me there's only one option.

There was only one option.

I lifted the lid of the square wooden waste bin I was lurking behind. It rose against the lights of the stage door, meaning I couldn't see what was inside. But I could smell it. A nauseating aroma of days-old Chinese food filled my nostrils. Just for a fleeting moment half of me asked the other half why I didn't get a proper job, but there wasn't time to find an answer.

There was just time to dive into the dark depths of hell, and close the lid behind me.

No matter what was waiting there to break my fall.

Chapter 16

My landing pad was every bit as horrific as my imagination had predicted. Hell described it pretty well. My feet squelched into a mess of stinking leftovers.

Sadly, it wasn't just my feet. As I bent over so the lid could close, half my body was immersed in piles of rotting, feted rubbish. I groaned to myself, the thought occurring to me that when morning came, I would grab the Chicago Tribune and find the situations vacant page.

But right then, I'd started the hell so I had to finish it. Close to the top of the bin the planks were separated. The half-inch crack gave me a good view of the stage door. Gritting my teeth, I pressed my eye to it and my nostrils together, and prayed desperately that it wouldn't be too long before my quarry emerged.

My prayers were half-answered. Just one minute later, people began to appear. The hood and the other guy smiled greetings to two of the girls, and they headed off towards the brightly-lit street, arms in arms. Five other girls came into my restricted view, and followed them quickly to the street.

None of them was Blondie.

Everything went quiet. Had I missed Nancy? No, the guy who had got to the stage door from the same direction as me was still there, the glow of a Lucky Strike burning between his nervous fingers. He was waiting for someone, and there could only be one someone. I looked him over, as best I could.

It didn't seem like he'd been shaving for very long. The less-than-expensive suit looked a little bit creased, and the fedora on his head was tipped back a little too far, emphasizing his lack of age. And the fact he was trying to be someone he wasn't. Clearly he was still in his late teens, and suffering from a bad case of hero worship for people who didn't deserve hero worship.

He sucked rapid draws from the cigarette in his fingers, doing his best to hold it in as masculine a way as he could, and looking like he was suffering from a bout of teenage impatience. I got the impression he wasn't too sure what reception to expect when the someone he was waiting for walked through the door.

He wasn't the only one suffering with impatience. My temporary apartment not only stank like what it actually was, the rubbish cocooning me was cold. Really cold. Which only served to make the nausea even more wretched, knowing most of it had been there in the freezing nights a lot longer than I had.

But then both our prayers were answered. Nancy finally appeared. Through the space in the planks, I could see and hear everything in the crisp night air.

'Geez Donnie, can't you take a hint?' she growled.

'Aw c'mon, Nancy... we can't leave it now. It won't be good for us, if you see what I'm saying.'

She narrowed her eyes at him. 'What do you mean?'

He put both his hands on her shoulders, in a desperate kind of way. 'Look baby... Mickey, he ain't happy, see? He already gave us half the cash, and we ain't delivering. And when Mickey ain't pleased, you know what that means.'

She shoved both her hands into his chest, knocking him back. 'You think I care, you lowlife bum? I've had it with you and your get-rich-quick schemes.' She swallowed hard, dropped her head for a moment, and then delivered the news. 'Donnie Caravello, we're over. So just get lost.'

92

'Baby... we can't be over. You and me, we're made for each other. And Mickey...'

'To hell with Mickey. If he puts a bullet in you, that's good riddance as far as I'm concerned. And I ain't your *baby*.'

Suddenly he looked agitated. Or scared out of his wits. '*Nanc*... Nanc, honey... you gotta listen to me. Ok, the plan failed, but she's gotta know where it is. Just coz you didn't get nowhere first time, it doesn't...'

'Ain't you listening to me, Donnie? I already told you, I went to see her in the cell, but then before we finished some old woman turned up...'

Old woman? I can't exactly say Nancy Pelowski was my favourite person, but that insult had instantly thrown her to the bottom of my pile...

'Baby... Nancy... you wanna be a hoofer the rest of your life? I...look, you got interrupted, but you gotta go see her again. Th... things depend on it...'

'How, brain of Chicago? Any moment now she'll be dispatched to Cook County, and it ain't so easy to fool people there.'

Donnie threw his hands in the air. 'I... maybe apply for a visiting order, say you're her sister or something?'

'You really think I'm a dumb Dora? She's African-American, you goof.'

'Half-sister?'

'Just get lost, Donnie.'

He looked like he was getting increasingly desperate. 'Baby, you can't high-hat me, not now.'

'Why? You in too deep to scram, lover boy?'

'We both is, Nanc.'

'Yeah, thanks to you.'

93

'Hey, don't do that. You was just as keen as me at first...
and you made all the moves, see?'

She let out a sarcastic laugh. 'Oh, I get the pitch now.
"*Nancy made all the running, I just went along with it?*"

He looked genuinely shocked. I guess I did too, but not at
Nancy's words. My attention was suddenly caught by
something a little closer to my current home. Something
furry, and snuffling ominously around my exposed leg.

I bit my lip... literally, trying not to scream. I guess I
should have anticipated it, having seen a few large city rats
scurrying away as I headed down the dark alley. Then again,
none of us had anticipated me ending up in an industrial
waste bin that hadn't been emptied for a couple of weeks.
Or that the leg in question would be smeared with days-old
Chinese food that was perfectly edible for a hungry rat.

I swallowed a little blood from the cut on my tongue,
and hoped my companion could tell the difference between
cold oriental food and warm human flesh.

Donnie was doing his best to contradict Nancy's
accusation. 'Baby, no... you know what this is about. A new
life in Florida, remember?'

She turned away, threw her hands against the wall
above her head, and then laid a weary head there too. 'I'm
beat, Donnie. Walk me home, please?'

'You just told me to get lost.'

'Sure... walk me home first, and then you can beat it.'

'Aw, Nanc...'

The two of them walked off together. I watched through
the crack until they reached the corner, and then threw
open the lid, gasping in fresh air. Luckily, the Chinese-food-
loving rat hadn't fancied female flesh, but it must have been
a close call. I stood up, covered in oriental slime, and

stretched my back, deciding I was getting too old for hiding in waste bins.

'Ho...'

A sudden cry next to me shook me back to harsh reality. A little Chinese chef was staring in shock at a sight he likely never thought he'd see, a bucket of food waste swinging from his left hand.

I stepped from my hell-hole as officially as I could, brushed some of the smelly crap from my person, and them swirled my equally-smelly scarf around my neck.

'City council inspectorate. Next time, get your bins emptied more often,' I growled as I headed off after my two quarries.

Chapter 17

In the length of time it had taken me to extract myself from the waste bin and reprimand the chef, the two lovebirds had disappeared. I headed quickly to the corner, and glanced along the brightly-lit street.

I spotted them a couple of hundred yards in front. It made my head shake. It had only taken them that two hundred yards to forgive and forget, and wrap their arms around each other's waists.

Kids.

Luckily it was almost eleven, and the kind of temperature to make most sensible people snuggle up in front of a log fire, so there weren't many pedestrians around. Even if there had been, people would have kept clear of me, the stench making sure I had my personal no-go zone.

I followed Nancy and Donnie five blocks away from The Loop, my surroundings slowly getting more residential. We'd just made a somewhat less-desirable part of the city when they climbed the steps of a tenement block, and stood a moment in front of the door.

I made a note of the address, although there was no way to know the apartment number. My trusty little notebook had escaped the worst of my plunge into the joys of the orient, but still somehow managed to possess more than a faint aroma of sweet and sour sauce.

I watched as they exchanged a few words, but I couldn't risk getting close enough to hear. Or risk tackling Blondie while she was in the company of an angst-ridden teenager.

Unless her name was on the doorbell panel, it looked like my night could be over. Once she high-hatted Donnie and disappeared through the door, I wouldn't know which bell to press.

Maybe I was getting too old for this game. Or more likely, I just didn't understand teenagers well enough. The next thing I knew, their lips met briefly, and then Nancy stuck her key in the door and opened it.

She disappeared inside. And so did Donnie.

Kids.

I turned away. I was hardly willing to hang around in my current state, and Donnie was hardly likely to leave until the light of morning anyway. It was time to make my smelly way home.

I would have loved to wave down a cab, but really? One look at my soy-sauce-ridden hair and one smell of my rancid body would have made any cab driver worth his salt screech away in a cloud of prairie dust.

There was no choice. It was a lengthy walk for me, dipping into dark doorways to avoid dark looks from pedestrians who were in a far better state than I was.

I couldn't remember ever being more grateful to reach home. As soon as I made the apartment I ripped off every item of clothing, and tied it all up in an old pillowcase. Tomorrow I would visit Chinese Charlie, who would guffaw out his infectious laugh when he realized I needed his laundry to remove the remains of food from his own country.

Naked, I threw on every cooking ring on the stove, and boiled up as much water as I could. And then finally I sank into the tub, and washed away the remains of the night.

It hadn't been the best of days, but I tried to compensate for the lingering oriental aromas by telling myself it had been a revealing one. Deliberately plunging into a vat of rancid food might not have been everyone's choice of finishing off a lovely evening, but it had brought its bonuses.

Like it had made it possible to overhear a conversation I wouldn't otherwise have done. Donnie and Nancy thought they were alone, and believed no one could hear their incriminating words. But thanks to a set of fortunate and unfortunate circumstances, I had overheard.

Perhaps it was the product of an overly-suspicious mind, but in my world what was said smacked of a seriously underhand scenario. They'd played Daphne to try and get hold of the mysterious key, but although what I'd heard made that clear, it raised a whole heap of other questions.

Donnie wasn't old enough or capable enough on his own of masterminding such a sting... but the mysterious Mickey probably was. He was also clearly capable of being scarily displeased that the key still hadn't been located.

The key to *what*?

And how did they persuade Daphne to murder the man she loved?

These were questions that were multiplications of previous questions. A few had been answered, but all it had done was to add more on the pile. I needed a key too... one that would unlock the million-dollar answer.

The one that seemed a million miles away.

I plunged my head under the water. The irony didn't escape me. It was a simple matter to lift it out again, run my hands through my hair, and blink my eyes clear.

But for both Daphne and me, getting our combined heads above the surface of cloudy waters was beginning to seem like a far harder task.

Chapter 18

The next morning, something was still telling my nostrils I stank of foul-smelling waste bins. It might have been purely psychological, but there was one way to find out. I said good morning to Archie, sitting my butt on the end of his desk for a minute or two so I was as close to him as I could manage without appearing too personal. I told him about my late evening and the conversation I'd overheard, deliberately omitting any facts about Chinese food.

He didn't say a word about rank smells in the air, and if Archie didn't remark about them in his own unique way, then they didn't exist anywhere else but my imagination.

A little relieved, I made my way to the station house, but this time not to see Daphne. There was nothing positive to tell her, and I assumed hearing about my altercation with a pile of greasy, rat-infested rubbish wouldn't be as important as her own impending altercation with the women of murderess row.

I needed to see Frank, and persuade him to allow me to do something he wouldn't think was a good idea.

I found the man at his desk, pen in hand, a mountain of paperwork between him and me.

'Wrapping-up early for Christmas, Frank?'

'Very funny,' he growled. 'But true, I guess.'

'Sometimes I wonder what happened to justice in this city. Then again, I'm not sure there ever really was any.'

He glanced up to me, his eyes heavy, and yet another cigar held between his nicotine-stained fingers. 'Can't see there's much doubt she's guilty, when all said and done.'

'Maybe. But there is a microscopic doubt... and a bigger chunk of doubt about who else was involved.'

'What you saying, Sandie?'

I realized I'd said too much, so hastily backtracked. 'Look Frank, I know you gotta toe the line, so it's best I don't say anymore right now. But I've got a request.'

He shook his head, already aware he wasn't going to like what he was about to hear. 'Go on,' he said wearily.

'James is dead, and Daphne is banged up for his murder. There's no one to look after their stuff. So Daphne has appointed me executor of her estate.'

'Really.'

'Sure. She told me you took her personal possessions off her when she got here, which included the house keys. I'd like them please, so I can go make a start.'

'Really.'

'You're saying *really* a lot, Frank.'

'That's coz I don't believe a word of it.'

'Are you saying I'm pulling your chain?'

'Sure I am.'

My hands seemed to throw themselves in the air, all by themselves. Frank knew me and my less-than-true stories a bit too well. 'Ok, so I am pulling your chain. But you have a heart, Frank, and I'm all Daphne's got now... and I've found out a couple of things to throw an underhand pitch at the batter.'

'What things?'

'As I said, right now you don't want to know. But I know you want to know.'

'But you're not telling me what I want to know.'

'I... look... just give me custody of the house keys, please?'

100

'Sandie, you know that's more than my job's worth, without an official document of execution.'

'Only if someone finds out. And I'm not telling anyone, trust me.'

'Trust you? You're a private investigator... and a female one too.'

I threw him a glare. 'Didn't take you for a misogynist, Frank.'

'Aw, geez... I'm not. Just trying to find an excuse not to do what you ask.'

'There aren't any excuses. It's the right thing to do, and you know it.'

'Right? It couldn't be wronger.'

'That's not a word. And who's going to feed the cat anyway?'

'What cat?'

'Um... the one Daphne might have.'

'Aw, geez...' He pulled open the bottom desk drawer, and lifted out a large paper bag. 'You know you're a pain in...'

'It's been said many times before, Frank. Mostly by you. Thank you.'

He shook his head, and handed me a small set of keys. There were just three on it, all of them looking like they opened outside doors. 'You bring these back first think in the morning, ok? And if you really want to be appointed as executor, get the right paperwork.'

'Will do, sir,' I grinned, and bolted from the station house, before Frank had a chance to change his mind.

'Grab your coat, Archie. And I don't just mean just to cover up that goddamn awful knitted waistcoat of yours.'

'Hey, boss. Don't be so disparaging. My mother made it.'

'Exactly.'

'Where are we going, like a prairie wind?'

'South Shore.'

'Geez, why are we going there?'

'That's the address on Daphne's key-ring.'

'How the hell... ok, I won't ask.'

'Don't fret, Archie. It's all above board. Well, kind of.'

He narrowed his eyes, and followed me down the stairs. Maybe he also knew me too well.

I filled him in with a few details as we took the tram-ride. I also missed out a few. But he had to know why we were heading to the home of his favourite fantasy. That wasn't too easy to explain either; I wasn't entirely sure why we were going.

I'd convinced myself the primary reason was to try and find the mysterious key, or at least a clue to why it was of such serious interest to a female 'bit on the side'.

That was true enough, but somehow my insatiable curiosity wanted to poke around Daphne's personal space, and maybe discover more about the gal, and the husband who was no more.

Seeing her in such a state, all my heart wanted to do was discover something to tell me just why she'd ended up in such a state. Talking with her so distraught and confused, I couldn't bring myself to ask her the million dollar question I really should have... *why* she'd done what she had.

Although after I'd thought about it, I realized I wouldn't have got much of an answer anyway. Daphne couldn't even *remember* doing it, so she sure wasn't going to tell me why.

The clues to the infuriating puzzle didn't lie within Daphne... they were lurking somewhere else, and no one was going to bother lifting the stones to see what was underneath except Archie and me.

102

Some kind of connection to the mob existed, that much was clear. It was a fair bet Blondie had some kind of connection too, wanted or unwanted. Desperate to find the mysterious key, she'd promised Daphne if she told her where it was, she'd be set free.

In an open-and-shut case, there weren't many people in Chicago powerful enough to wield that much clout. And even less of them were honest citizens.

One burning question was sparking to a peak of flame in my mind. Had the curly blonde simply not anticipated the tragic outcome? Or had she somehow *caused* it?

It was doubtful our current destination would reveal an answer to that. But we had to start somewhere.

Chapter 19

Archie let out a whistle as we stood on the sidewalk, gazing across at the elegant white-painted house.

'Was this part of your fantasy?' I grinned to him.

'Sure puts it in perspective... um, *what* fantasy?'

'Shall we go inside, let you live it a little more?'

'You're disgusting,' he retorted, making for the front door.

The detached two-storey house wasn't quite the finest in the street, but it sure put most people's dwellings to shame. Built to emulate the Romanesque style of a bygone era, a large pillared entranceway was raised off the small front garden a few steps. It looked like a mini White House.

Well-manicured lawns surrounded the place, interspersed with equally well-trimmed ornamental bushes, and the occasional tree that had survived the housing development of a few years ago. Neo-classical window frames interrupted a plain white façade, which was topped by a grey slate roof with three dormer windows poking out of it.

A small graveled drive made up most of the small front garden. There was no car parked there, but I noticed the drive ran around the side of the house to a garage that looked as big as most Chicagoan's houses.

Archie was already at the art-deco front door, peering through the small panes of the narrow floor-to-ceiling windows each side of it. Still he looked impressed. 'Go on then, unlock it,' he said impatiently.

I fumbled with the keys, a small part of me feeling a little dirty. If things went the way the city chiefs wanted, Daphne would never get to see the inside of it again… but even so, that little gremlin was telling me I was violating her privacy.

I shook it away. If it wasn't me, it would soon enough be someone who was even more of a stranger. It had to be me.

Everything was white. As we walked hesitantly through the door, the sheer whiteness hit me straightaway. Apart from the small black floor tiles dotted around the white floor, and the black handrail topping the white balustrades, everything was as dazzling as Daphne's smile.

Archie whistled again, as I took stock of my monochrome surroundings. Several doors with semi-circular tops led off the entrance hall, but a set of double doors looked like they gave access to the main living area. All the doors were closed. I pointed to the twin doors, and we walked over to them, dropped the handle, and stepped through.

It *was* the main living area, and just as white as the hallway. Apart from the greenery of large potted palms, and the black and gold of the drapes caressing the three arched windows overlooking the much-larger rear garden, everything was a multitude of shades of white.

I heard myself let out a gasp, but it was nothing to do with the décor. Archie looked at me with a deep frown on his freckled brow.

'Looks like the maid hasn't been for a while,' he said, in a choked kind of way.

Maybe the maid hadn't, but clearly someone had. And very recently too.

Nothing was where it should be. Everything that could be ransacked was littered across the floor, making it look like a hurricane had swept through the place. But it was no natural disaster that had blasted its way in. Someone had been looking for something, and they hadn't cared too much about what they disturbed to find it.

Daphne's lovely home was a bombsite.

I shook away the desolation, and glanced to the windows. One of them was a set of double doors leading to the garden. And they were open, shards of glass littering the white carpet where someone had smashed their way in.

'Archie, let's split up, search the rest of the house. And be careful. All the interior doors are closed, so they're likely long gone, but you never know.'

He nodded, and headed to one of the other doors. I climbed the stairs, but my heart was still on the ground floor. Daphne's world had already crumbled to dust... this was the short straw she really didn't need.

But as I checked the bedrooms, and found every one wrecked, the thought occurred to me it might be the proverbial short straw, but it could be the one that repaired the camel's back, not broke it.

Someone was desperate to find something. Whether they did or didn't, it was a pretty fair indication all was not as cut-and-dried as it appeared.

A shout from the ground floor ripped me away from the devastation. I forced heavy legs to take me back down the stairs, and found Archie in James's office. Judging by the hundreds of books scattered over the floor, it had doubled as a kind of library.

He was holding a book in his hand, and looking at me like he didn't quite believe he was. 'He's got every Charles Dickens novel here, by the looks of it,' he said slowly. 'I just happened to pick this one off the floor.'

I looked at the green book in his hands, *A Tale of Two Cities.* The irony of it wasn't lost on me. 'I guess Dickens wasn't referring to New York and Chicago… but hey, if you want to read it, no one's going to miss it.'

'That's not what I'm saying,' he said. 'Already read it anyway.'

'But you're obviously trying to tell me something, or you wouldn't be waving it at me.'

'Yeah I am. Whoever ransacked the place opened the cover of each book, looking to see if something was hidden inside.'

'Some kind of note?'

'Nah. They looked inside the cover, but they didn't look *inside.*'

'Archie, I know it happens a lot, but you're not making sense.'

He handed me the book. 'Yeah I am. Look inside… properly.'

I flicked open the front and back cover. Nothing that wasn't supposed to be there jumped up and hit me in the face. Archie was still grinning encouragement to me, so I flicked the pages with my thumb, like a card sharp shuffling a deck.

Then Archie's words finally made sense. Right in the middle of the pages, I saw something that definitely shouldn't have been there. 'How the hell, Archie? You got a sixth sense I don't know about?'

He shook his head, like he couldn't believe it himself. 'Unfortunately, no. Pure chance… I picked this up, and just flicked through the pages. I don't even know why.'

'Maybe because you're a genius?'

'Aw boss… you're too kind.'

It was my turn to shake my head, as I placed the open book on what was left of the desk, like it was made of solid gold. It quite possibly could be.

107

In the middle of the book, a few pages had something missing. James had carefully cut out a small rectangle, just big enough to hold what was taped inside the hollow.

It was a small, flat key. Just a simple piece of stamped out metal, unremarkable other than the fact a luxury house had been wrecked by those who had failed to find it.

I eased it away from the tape holding it in place, and held it up so we could both see it.

'Doesn't look like much, does it, Archie?'

'No, but what it unlocks could for sure be very much.'

He was right, to the point of possibly serious understatement. As I turned it around in my fingertips, a couple more jigsaw pieces fell into place. I knew exactly what it unlocked. I'd seen similar keys before, owned by one or two of my better-off clients.

It was the key to a safe deposit box.

Chapter 20

Archie and me made our way back to town, the precious key hidden away in the secret inside pocket of my coat. Archie had steam coming out of his ears.

'Seems to me that key holds the... key, if you get me, Sandie.'

'Yeah, the power to wreck houses and lives, amongst other things.'

'Except it's not the key itself, just what it unlocks.'

'But what does it unlock, Archie? Still waiting for your genius brain to tell me.'

He shook his head, his genius suddenly failing him. 'Well, it's a safe deposit box, but... maybe a hell of a lot of money, or jewelry?'

'It would make sense, if someone found out it existed. But even Daphne didn't know.'

'Well, she *told you* she didn't know.'

'You didn't see her, Arch. She wasn't sure what day it was, let alone have the ability to tell me lies.'

'Still think she must have known.'

I wasn't convinced. There was one other possibility. 'James might have kept it to himself to protect her.'

'Make sense. But if he did, he must also have known there was a possibility of nasty things happening to him. Now that they have, how was he going to let her know the riches in the safe deposit box existed, if he didn't?'

I threw my eyes to the metal tram roof. Archie made a good point. Daphne had no idea he held a deposit box, or which bank it was in. Just the box number and WSB was stamped on the key. Somehow, James must have left her a clue only she would recognize, so that if the worst happened she could find something she didn't know existed. But how?

One more point of tragic irony thumped into my brain. If James was concerned his life was at risk, he sure never expected it to end at the hands of his own wife.

The second point of nauseating fear churning my stomach was that Archie and me had suddenly become unique human beings. We were the only two people alive who knew where the deposit box was.

I now knew for sure what James was doing when I followed him four nights ago.

And that made the simple piece of metal hidden on my person a red hot commodity.

We didn't go straight back to the office. We had to return the keys, and Frank needed to be informed a home-wrecking had occurred. And I had to be sure what was left of Daphne's stuff would be respected.

He threw his hands in the air as I told him of the devastation we'd found. 'Geez Sandie… you're a pain…'

'Yeah, yeah, I know. But just get your frustrations into gear, Frank. I only found the aftermath, I didn't have anything to do with it.'

He slumped down behind his desk, buried his face in his hands. 'Sure… sorry. Not your fault… this time.'

I handed him back the keys. 'Maybe it was a good job it was Archie and me who found the break-in. If anyone else had been left to clean up, they would have likely just thrown everything in a dumpster.'

He peeped at me from between his fingers. 'That's what we'd usually do too, Sandie.'

'But you're not going to, not this time, are you?'

'I guess you're going to tell me.'

110

'You know me too well. So out of respect for Daphne, and the fact I'm discovering things that shed new light on the cut-and-dried obvious, how about we show a little compassion for now, and get what remains of her stuff packed up carefully, and put in storage?'

He shook his head, but seemed to reluctantly agree. 'We got a cleaner team here, who go in and make good... usually after messy gangland killings, admittedly. I could use them.'

'Sounds good. But I've got one more request.'

'Go on,' he said, in the resigned fashion that was becoming his norm.

'Again out of respect for Daphne, I want Archie to go with the cleaner team, and make sure her stuff is removed with care and consideration. This might be mob-related, but in that way it isn't.' I glanced over to Archie. 'That ok with you, Peanut?'

He seemed to be grinning. 'Sure thing, boss.'

I had little doubt he would. Overseeing the removal of every single thing his fantasy possessed wouldn't exactly seem like work to him.

Frank finally looked at me with his full face. 'What about you, Sandie? Won't you want to be there too?'

'You need to get your guys in the house sharp, Frank. It's the end of the day now and too late, but tomorrow morning will have to do. Unfortunately I've got places to be, so Archie will be in charge on this one... if that's ok with you, of course.'

He let out the deep sigh that was also becoming familiar. 'As you are well aware, I gotta keep this in-house right now, until you bring me conclusive evidence someone else is to blame. Daphne is at Cook now, and as far as the authorities know, she's only going to come out of there in a box. So it's still down to you guys, coz I can't be seen to be doing nothing to contravene that.'

'You're a star, Frank.'

'Sure I am. And you're a pain in... well, you know. I don't suppose you're going to tell me where you gotta be in the morning that's so urgent?'

'Come on, Frank. The less you know, and all that?'

He waved us away, knowing he wasn't going to get any more out of me. He was right. He still didn't know where James had gone four nights ago, or that we'd actually found the key that might turn out to be *the key*.

It was better that way, for all of us.

I parted company with Archie outside the station house. The sun was sinking below the skyline, and it was time we were both relaxing with a good book. Preferably, one without a part of its pages missing.

I headed back to the apartment, a mix of anticipation and dread whirring around my cogs. The key in my pocket was slowly burning its way through to my gut, and making it tighten with fear. That tiny, seemingly-innocent piece of metal seemed to be the hottest commodity in Chicago right then, and one that a certain someone would stop at nothing to get hold of.

It wasn't lost on me that I had no idea who that someone was... or what was in the box the key would open. Both of those harsh facts of life were crucial to finding the real key... the one that opened Daphne's cell door on Murderess Row.

My first port of call in the morning was the Wallace and Simpson bank. I had the key to the safe deposit box someone else owned, but I suspected that without a letter of authority from its dead owner, I would be refused official access.

Even so, I had to try. Finding out what was in that box was essential.

Chapter 21

My suspicions were well-founded. I had as much hope of getting near that box as flying to the moon.

The manager who looked every bit like the bank manager in a Charles Dickens novel wasn't having any of it. He took me aside to a quiet corner of the foyer, and slammed me down in his prim official way.

'I'm very sorry... Mrs. deMountford, but Mr. deMountford has given me extremely strict instructions that no one other than himself or his wife is allowed access to his box.'

'But I am his wife.'

His bushy eyebrows lifted annoyingly as he looked through the thin file in his hands. 'I'm sorry, but I can't accept your proliferations, madam.'

'Excuse me? Look, he always preferred older women, don't you see... sir?'

'That may be so, madam, but you do not match the description I have been given.'

'Well... life has been hard this last year.'

'Really.'

'Are you telling me I'm trying to deceive you, sir? I have the key.'

He shook his head in a disparaging kind of way, and turned the file so I could see it. 'Well, unless this *hard year* has both aged you, and changed the colour of your skin, then there is nothing I can do.'

I glanced in horror at the photograph of James and Daphne he'd obviously given the manager. 'Ah.'

'Yes indeed. *Ah*, whoever you are.'

'Ok, look, I'm Daphne's friend. She's incar... incapacitated at the moment. She asked me to come on her behalf.'

He shook his head, in a very final kind of way. 'I'm sorry. Unless you have a signed letter of permission, or are accompanied by Mr. or Mrs. deMountford, there is nothing I can do,'

I knew I wasn't getting anywhere, but there was something he didn't know. 'Mr. deMountford is no longer with us. He lost his life five nights ago.'

The bushy eyebrows raised. 'I see. May I ask how?'

'Um... a mob killing.'

'Well... that puts a new light on it.'

I looked at him in faint hope. 'So you'll allow me to retrieve the contents of the box then?'

He wasted no time in slamming me back down. 'Oh no, that can't happen. But if you come back with Mrs. deMountford...'

I left the bank. I could have told him James's wife was currently languishing on Murderess Row for killing him, but I doubted it would make any difference to the brick wall James had erected. And I really didn't want to give a stranger all the gruesome facts.

No doubt he'd read about it in the Tribune before too long anyway.

There was only one way I was going to get to slip the key in that particular lock, and it wasn't exactly the easiest thing in the world. I had to clear Daphne's name, so she could be released and visit the bank with me.

Still no pressure then.

I wasn't exactly sure why, but something forced my legs in the direction of James's office. I doubted there would be much there to help the cause, but it was the only place associated with the deMountfords I hadn't visited. Not internally, anyway.

Inside the building, the foyer was just as unremarkable as the outside. I took the elevator to the fourth floor, and as the doors pinged aside, looked for an entrance that I hoped would be marked with his name. Just before I found it, it occurred to me it would likely be locked. As far as I knew James worked alone, so when he wasn't there he would be foolish to leave it open.

I found his door, a small plaque with his name telling me it was his. It wasn't locked. Locking it actually wasn't possible, when the part of the door frame that contained the latch plate had been smashed away.

My stomach churned. Discovering places belonging to the deMountfords that had been ransacked was becoming a habit.

A piece of string tied to a nail was keeping the door from swinging open. I untied it, and walked hesitantly inside. Somehow I knew it would be reminiscent of what we'd found in their white house.

I was right. It was exactly like the white house. I gazed around at the all-too-familiar devastation, my heart thumping like a Studebaker piston engine. The tornado that had also singled out James's office wouldn't bother him anymore, but it was sure troubling those who were left alive.

Those who knew why it had arrived, anyway.

I was just about to search for... something, when a hesitant voice spoke from behind me. 'Hello... are you from the police?'

I spun round, and saw a young woman. She looked quite delicate, and well-dressed for the white-collar worker she clearly was. She stood in the doorway, a half-smile on her face, her hands clasped together in front of the white patterned blouse. She looked like a secretary, or a personal assistant of some kind.

'Um… I'm a detective… a private investigator. And you are..?'

'Oh, I see. I'm Velma Williams. I work in the next office along. Such a terrible thing…'

'What happened here, Velma?'

'Oh… don't you know?'

'Mrs. deMountford has asked me to find out… see if I can unearth anything to help.'

She nodded, a little like a frightened mouse. 'Well, two mornings ago I was the first in, and found… this. The door smashed in, and everything… where it shouldn't be. I called the police; they came and poked around a bit, then left. They seemed to think it wasn't worth their time, as James hadn't reported anything. But no one's been here for the last two days, so I can't say any more, I'm afraid.'

She had to know. 'James is dead, Velma.'

Her hands flew to her cheeks. 'Oh no… he was such a gentleman… how..?'

'That's what I'm investigating. I can't really say anymore right now.'

She dabbed her eyes, let out a little sob. 'Oh, this is so distressing. I don't know what to do.'

'Please, Velma, don't do anything right now. The authorities are taking care of it. I'm sorry… sorry for your loss.'

She looked tearful and distressed. 'I would never have thought… *James*…'

117

'Yes, I know. It's been a shock to us all. Is there anything else you can think of to tell me?'

She shook her head vigorously. 'No, not really. After the police left, I waited for James or his assistant to come, but they didn't arrive. Then just before I went home I tied the door, because no one else had. I'm sorry I can't be more help.'

'Wait... his *assistant*? I didn't think he had an assistant?'

'Oh yes, just for two days a week. He helped James with his filing. But I haven't seen him since... since this happened. I don't know what's going on.'

I was picking up a nasty little metaphoric piece of the jigsaw from the floor. It was dirty, and trampled on. 'This assistant, did he have a name?'

'Oh, I never really knew his full name. James called him Donald, that's all I know.'

I thanked her, and left the devastation behind. Quite why Frank hadn't told me James's office had been broken into was as much of a mystery as anything else. The only thing that came to mind was that he actually didn't know.

For sure Downtown was handled by a different precinct, but I would have thought some sharing of information would have occurred, given the blatant connection.

Unless someone in a high place wanted it kept quiet.

My heart was still thumping. The totally-innocent Velma had handed me one more glaring coincidence. James had a part-time assistant. He clearly wouldn't be privy to the seedier side of James's work for Capone, which was conducted out of his, and most other people's sight.

But the brightly-lit sign flashing its dazzle into my brain was telling me that somehow this assistant did discover something about James's secret.

118

Velma hadn't known his surname. But his first name was Donald. A name truncated by mates and girlfriends to *Donnie*.

Chapter 22

I sipped my coffee in a deliberately thoughtful kind of way. Frank, sitting opposite me in the Uptown café, did the same. It was his suggestion, after I'd told him there were a few more unpleasant facts he should be aware of.

It seemed he already knew they weren't for public consumption.

Archie and the cleaner crew had spent the day sorting out the devastation at the white house. What hadn't already been destroyed had been packed in boxes, and stored temporarily, and quietly, in a spare basement room at the station house. That, at least, had been taken care of.

His nimble fingers had also managed to access the safe. What passed as *cash for expenses* in Daphne's now nonexistent world had been hidden away on his person, without the cleaner crew knowing it had.

A couple of thousand dollars was now sitting in the back of my filing cabinet, ready for when, and if Daphne was ever able to make use of it.

He also discovered a Studebaker roadster in the garage. He'd told the house rental agent it would be collected in the next few days.

It was fortunate Archie was there. He was able to deal with the guy who'd turned up just after lunch, proclaiming to be the renting agent. He'd checked him out, there and then.

He *was* the renting agent. It seemed the deMountfords didn't own the dazzling property they lived in. Which led me to believe my favourite couple weren't as well off as they'd wanted people to think.

It might explain Daphne's desire to resurrect her career as a dancer and actress. And James's decision to work for the mob.

Frank ripped my thoughts away. 'This is turning into a huge pile of stinking crap, Sandie.'

'You think Devey's behind it?'

'Someone high up is. There ain't no record of any office break-ins Downtown. That's dodgy in itself, seeing as you was told the police there got involved.'

'Seems even you only get to know what they want you to know, Frank.'

He nodded his head sadly. 'Ain't no room these days for an old cop who never took back-handers.'

I could feel his dejection. And it matched my own. 'This city is becoming the property of those who aren't too bothered about how they get to own it, that's a raging certainty.'

'Maybe the sooner I give it all up the better, hey Sandie?'

'Don't say that, Frank. What would I do without you? What would the few decent people left do either?'

'Sure, but sometimes I wonder if the stress is worth the dedication.'

'Maybe we should just bus all the good people out of town, and leave Chicago to the mob. See how long it takes them to kill each other.'

He laughed, mirthlessly. 'Even then, somehow I get the feeling Capone will come out on top.'

I nodded thoughtfully again. 'He's got to be behind this. He found out James was hiding away a fortune, but he still doesn't know where.'

'That don't make sense either. James was killed in Capone's favourite gin joint, while he was there. Can you explain that?'

121

The desolate, vaguely desperate feeling was there again. 'No, I can't. And it's starting to drive me crazy. I've found several pieces of the jigsaw, but every time I think they're fitting together, I find one lug isn't quite where it should be. It's not a nice feeling, Frank.'

He finished his coffee, and put a hand on my arm. 'Sandie, you be careful, please. This whole thing is getting murkier than a sewage farm. You tread delicate, ok?'

I wrapped my hand around his. 'Like a baby mouse, Frank. And thank you for being my rock. I know your hands are tied on this one, but you still seem to be able to grasp a string or two.'

He shook his head again. 'Doing my best, gal, but as you say, I gotta rely on you more than you rely on me. If I live, I kinda want to be able to *live*, if you get me?'

'I get you, Frank. You keep your powder dry, for me. But I've got one more favour to ask... and you're not going to like this one either.'

'Getting used to it, Sandie. Just lay it on me.'

'If you're not too busy in the morning, I'd like to go see Daphne. Calling in to Cook County with you by my side will make it seem more official. I can play Nancy's card, and say I'm her attorney. If you're there to back me up, it won't seem so far-fetched.'

'You know what? I'm past caring. As it happens I gotta go see someone incarcerated there, a totally unconnected case, so it ain't no hassle. If it gets out I'm colluding with a private investigator against the wishes of the city though, that's the end of my career... but what the hell.'

'It won't get out, Frank. Not from me, anyway. I've just got some fresh questions for Daphne, based on what we've discovered in the last day or so. She might be able to help drop another piece of the jigsaw into place... but I'm not asking you to put your career too much at risk. It's your call, really.'

He stood up. 'You want the truth? I need to get one over on this web of corruption just as much as you do. I'll pick you up at ten, and get you into Murderess Row... the rest is up to you.'

I watched him walk slowly away, a little more stooped than I remembered. A decent man with a heart, he was being slowly devoured by the gathering masses of those who were quite prepared to save their own skins by not seeing things as honestly as he did.

I had to make sure we put the last pieces of the puzzle in their right places, before the prairie vultures stripped him to his bones.

Chapter 23

The impressive Romanesque façade of the court building filled the windscreen as we drove slowly past on Michigan Avenue, and threw a left into Dearborn Street. Past the almost-as-impressive residential staff quarters building, we made another left into Illinois Street, and came to a stop outside the less elegant Cook County jail entrance.

As we stepped out of the car into the chilly early-winter sunshine, Frank threw me a nervous smile. I couldn't see any humour in it. 'You got that fake card ready, um... Nancy?'

'In my hand, Frank.'

He nodded, clearly not that impressed with what I'd persuaded him to do. 'Let's do this, then,' he said, the nod turning into a shake.

'Sure Frank, but one thing... stop looking as guilty as everyone locked up inside, please?'

He laughed. 'You kidding me? Not one of them looks as guilty as me, coz according to them, they're all innocent.'

I acknowledged his correction as we walked into reception. 'Bad choice of words, I guess. Just look like the officer of the law you are then, ok?'

He switched on his official face, and headed to the man behind the desk, who clearly knew him. 'Hey Frank, here to see Joe Capaldi again?' he said flatly. 'Who's the dame?'

Frank narrowed his eyes, but didn't retort about his description of me. 'This here *dame* is Nancy Pelowski, Daphne de Mountford's attorney. She'd like a word with her please, while I interview Capaldi.'

I handed the man my card. He glanced at it like he really couldn't be bothered, and picked up the phone. Frank led me away to the far side of the room. 'Looks like you got your wish, Sandie. In a couple of minutes we'll both be taken to the respective blocks. Just be prepared for the lowest of the low, ok? It ain't exactly high society in here.'

'Kind of figured that out, Frank.'

'Yeah, but you ain't *seen* it yet.'

I swallowed hard, wondering just what I'd let myself in for. I'd mentally prepared myself for a hard tug on the emotions, telling myself no matter what I saw, Daphne was experiencing it far worse, and for far longer than me. Regardless, Frank's words had made me sit up and take notice, and wonder if I'd gone far enough on the road to mental preparation.

I didn't have too long to swallow hard. Two people walked through a door from the rest of the jail. One was a man, who obviously knew Frank. He nodded to me as they disappeared through the door.

The other was a woman. She was short, a little tubby, and looked like a prisoner. A one-piece jail suit adorned her diminutive body, and her curly white hair gave away the fact she was no spring chicken, and had likely been a part of the Cook County female division for a very long time. The only thing that distinguished her from an inmate was the prison crest on her chest, with the word 'Matron' sewn in below it.

'You here to see deMountford, they tell me,' she said curtly.

I held out my fake card, but she ignored it. 'You'd better come with me then,' she growled as she turned for the door, anticipating that I would follow.

I did follow. 'I'm Nancy, by the way. Pleased to meet you.'

She stopped striding, turned and looked at me with dead, dark eyes. 'Sure, honey. You get fifteen minutes, ok? There ain't the luxury of a carpeted interview room in Murderess Row, so you'll have to conduct whatever business you got in her cell. Which ain't gonna be easy.'

'I'm sorry. I'm not sure what you mean?'

She turned away again, and I saw a slight shake of the silver curls. 'The cells are open-fronted. It's quiet right now, just five other inmates. You'll still have to do your best to ignore the heckles, ok?'

We walked through into the guard room. The woman lifted up the large set of keys dangling from the black belt around her waist, and shoved one of them into the lock of a steel door. I asked her name.

'Matron Irene Morston. I take care of these gals. Some more than others, if you get me.'

'Sure. Guess it depends how well-heeled they are.'

She glanced up to me, the eyes narrowed. 'You not been in Chicago long then?'

'All my life, actually.'

'Geez, you must be one of them Temperance do-gooders.'

'No. You saw my card.'

'Sure. And you're in for an eye-opener, Nancy, or whatever your name is. Although I'm not surprised the likes of her can afford a lawyer. I *am* surprised you're a woman though, given there must be a dozen male attorneys desperate to get her off. Negro or otherwise.'

'You're being insulting to my client, Miss Morston. Are you racially prejudiced?' I asked, as a genuine thumping became blatantly obvious in my chest. She wasn't convinced I was who I was purporting to be, but it still wasn't stopping her letting me in. She likely didn't care. But I did care, about the derogatory words she'd used, and what I was apparently about to experience.

Suddenly I felt like a fly, about to get trapped in a spider's web.

The cries started as soon as Irene locked the door again behind us. My heart sank, and not just because of the desperation in the voices. We were in a long high-ceilinged corridor of a room, on a bare concrete floor the builders hadn't taken too much time to make smooth beneath our feet. High above our heads were four windows, the sills easily twenty feet above the floor. They were big, some five feet wide and maybe twelve feet tall.

No one was ever going to be able to use those to escape.

To our right was a run of twelve cells with steel-barred frontages. From what little I could see they looked small, not much light getting through from the high windows. As we ran the gauntlet to where Daphne's cell was located at the far end of the run, the inmates seemed pleased to see me.

'Hey, lady, you a brief? How about you get me set free too?'

'Might have known she'd get preferential treatment.'

'Goddamn blacks, thinking they's better than us. Go to hell, I say.'

'Hey, you a goody-two-shoes? I'm innocent, see? I shouldn't be here.'

The girl in the fifth cell didn't say a word, just stared at me through the one-inch thick bars. Fired up by what I heard from the other inmates and their warden, I glared at her pretty young face, almost spoiling for a fight.

'Don't you have anything to say?' I hissed.

127

Irene Morston pulled me away. 'She's Spanish. Don't speak a word of English. Ain't no trouble either. She's got a date with the electric chair next week though, so she won't be here much longer.'

'Do you actually sleep at night?' I growled at her.

She laughed in a dismissive kind of way, and shoved one of her multitude of keys into a cell door. 'It's a dirty job, honey, but if I don't do it, someone else a lot less understanding will. You got fifteen minutes with your floozy, remember? Not a minute longer.'

She walked away, heading back to her guard room, totally disinterested. It occurred to me if I bunged her a few dollars, Daphne might get a tender loving perk or two.

She needed some. As I turned to look at her, she let out a little, desolate sob.

I thought my heart had sunk to the floor when I first walked into the jail. Suddenly seeing Daphne deMountford, I realized it still had a way to go.

Chapter 24

Daphne's new home measured eight by six. Her temporary furnishings consisted of a hard, unforgiving bed, with a tiny, tatty nightstand next to it. A dingy lamp stood on its top, which for sure didn't work after lights-out. The only other item in the room was an open toilet, which looked more like a bucket without a lid.

It didn't feel much like her white house.

She ran to me, threw shaking arms around me, and buried her face in my shoulder. I held her tight, and then remembered who I was supposed to be, so eased her away.

'Hey, I know you're glad to see me, but I'm your lawyer, so getting hugged isn't conducive to good business, ok? And we've got a whole fifteen minutes, so we're not exactly wallowing in free time.'

She turned away, and wiped the tears from her cheeks. Dressed in a brown prison one-piece, she looked a shadow of the elegant woman I met a week ago. 'I'm sorry. It's just so good to see someone.'

'Yeah, I can imagine. No opportunistic lawyers come to call then?'

She looked at me with glossed eyes. 'Just one guy. He didn't stay long, when he realized what colour my skin is.'

I shook my head, even more desolately than I'd been getting used to. 'He'd likely want to sleep with you before taking on your case anyway.'

She let out another sob, and ran slender hands across her tear-stained face. 'Seems I'm a lost cause. No one's going to save me from the chair, are they?'

'Hey, you need to stop talking like that. And you need to stop lying to me, if we're going to stand any chance of getting you off this.'

She slumped down onto the hard mattress. 'I didn't lie to you, Sandie.'

'Maybe not, but you didn't tell me the truth, did you?'

'Not all of it, no.'

'You want to tell me why?'

She buried her face in her hands. 'Because if I did, you would have shown me the door. You told me as much.'

'Yeah, I did, didn't I?'

She had a relevant question for me. 'But you found out anyway, and still you haven't run a mile.'

I lowered my head, knowing that of all the things she'd said and not said, that was the truest. And it was the hardest to answer. I tried anyway.

'Maybe I have an aversion to injustice, which turned out to be stronger than my aversion to the mob.'

'Injustice? It seems I killed the man I loved. Surely that's the injustice here?'

'If you did kill him.'

She looked at me, her eyes narrowed to slits. 'Please don't say things just to make me feel better, Sandie. No matter what happened, the authorities will make sure an AA goes down for it.'

'Not if Frank and me have anything to do with it. He's the one good cop left in this city, by the way.'

'But it seems I did it.'

'You still can't remember?'

She shook her head. 'It all happened so fast. I've been over it a million times in my head. All I can remember is walking back through the bar entrance with Nancy by my side, and seeing James at the bar. I know I heard three gunshots, and then I looked down, and the gun was in my hand. *My own gun*, Sandie. No matter how hard I try and make sense of it, I can't see any.'

'Being off your face that night didn't help.'

Her head lowered to the uneven floor. 'I know. And that doesn't make sense either. I know my limits, and I've never gone beyond those before. So why that night?'

'There might be a reason.'

'Are you going to share?'

I told her a nutshell version of everything that had happened since the fateful night. It didn't seem she took it too well, the tears rolling down her cheeks. I guess the discoveries I'd made were positive ones in a way, but in another way, they were even more depressing.

My words had changed her perspective. She'd gone from not being able to remember pulling the trigger, to realizing that for whatever reason, she'd been set up.

Neither of us knew how. And that wasn't helping.

'Look, Daphne, we're running out of time. The matron will be back in five minutes, and that'll be it for now. I need to ask you some quick-fire questions, and I need honest, simple answers, ok?'

She nodded. I drew a deep breath. 'We know your white house was rented. Does that mean you're not as rich as you're making out?'

'We managed to leave England with some cash. But not as much as we would have liked. That's why we both got work... well, I tried to, as you know. A while ago we bought a house on the lake, but it's little more than a tumbledown shack. It needs a lot of time and money spent on it, which isn't going to happen now. The rental was to give us somewhere to live that kept up appearances. Back when

131

James met Capone in New York, the money was already dwindling, and his offer was too good for James to refuse.'

'Becoming his bookkeeper?'

'Yes. For ages he didn't tell me who he was working for... a bit ashamed, I suppose. Then finally he had to. I wasn't happy, but, well, needs must I suppose.'

'So when Capone relocated to Chicago, you did too?'

Daphne nodded, and I took a second to beat myself up. I already knew they'd all arrived at the same time, and failed to put two-and-two together. If I had, I wouldn't have been talking to Daphne in a Cook County jail cell.

But *she* would still have been there. With no one on her side.

I consoled myself with the thought I had done the right thing by her. It didn't help my personal dread so much, but it was still a valid argument.

'Did you know James had an assistant?'

'Not really. He said he had someone who kept his files in order on occasions, but I assumed it was one of the staff already in the building. You don't think..?'

'Oh yeah, I do. Donnie somehow discovered what James was doing, but clearly didn't have all the details. But he knew enough to realize whatever it was held significant value. He also knew he needed help to get hold of it, so he contacted this Mickey guy, whoever the hell he is, and roped in his girlfriend, Nancy. Sorry.'

Daphne threw her hands in the air. 'It's ok. I know I was a fool. She never really meant anything. It was just a bit of innocent fun.'

'Not so innocent, as it turns out.'

Her head lowered. 'No.'

'Ok, any minute now our dear matron will be back. You need to know the authorities are never going to be swayed by circumstantial evidence. The city bosses have already convicted you in their minds, and they'll not hang around making an example of you. *We* know you were set up, but somehow we've got to prove it. Conclusively. Without that, you're...'

'A dead woman.'

Again, I couldn't lie to her. 'Putting it simply, yes. But you need to know you have good friends on the side of the actual law. On *your* side. Just hold onto that, and know we're doing everything we can to make it right. But you've also got to understand I can't make wild promises of freedom, not in this city. If you were white-skinned, and had a Billy Flynn on your side, you'd be dancing into the sunset. But you're not, and you haven't. So sadly you're stuck with me and mine.'

'Billy Flynn? Isn't he the lawyer in Watkins' play?'

'Yes, an amalgamation of two real-life lawyers. In *Chicago*, he's one guy. One pretty despicable guy, if I'm honest.'

We heard the key turn in the cell-block door. Our time was up. Daphne threw me a scared-to-death look. 'I need a hug, but it's too late now. Please Sandie, do your best. I have faith.'

'That much I can promise.' I wrapped my hand around hers, just for a fleeting moment before a curt voice came from the other side of the bars.

'Time's up, lady.'

133

Chapter 25

It went against the grain, but as matron and me reached her guard room, I did something that was contrary to all my decent beliefs.

I gave her ten dollars, and told her to make Daphne's life as comfortable as she could... maybe with a few Lucky Strikes.

It was James's money after all, and if he was alive he would feel just as bad about Daphne's plight as I did.

At least, that's what I told myself.

I met Frank in reception, and we headed away from the hell-hole. 'You ok?' he asked me.

'Not really. I thought I'd prepared myself, but...'

'Grim, I know. Did you get anything useful?'

'Just confirmation Daphne has been set up. But we still don't know how they made it happen, or why.'

He nodded knowingly, and a little sadly. 'I don't need to tell you the city authorities ain't gonna budge unless we can present irrefutable evidence she was set up. The word scapegoat comes to mind.'

'No, you don't need to tell me, Frank. And somehow it's got to be soon, because I doubt they're going to hang around bringing her to a token trial.'

He didn't say any more. The look on his face was enough.

It was just past lunchtime when Frank dropped me back at the office. Archie, desperate his favourite fantasy lived on for him to dream another day, looked at me inquisitively.

'Nothing to report, Peanut, except what Daphne said just confirmed she's been set up.'

He looked upset, just before his head dropped to his chest. 'You gotta make this right, Sandie.'

'You stating the obvious again? But it might be *we* who have to set it right.'

'I'm just an office boy. What can I do?'

I put a caring hand on his shoulder. 'Archie, you're more than that. You found the key, didn't you? So maybe I need your incisive brain to see something I can't. Although what that might be, I don't have a clue.'

'Barnstorming session then?' he grinned.

'Bring your peanuts. You might need brain food.'

I poured Archie a glass of real whisky to go with his peanuts, and one for myself. It seemed like we both deserved it, and I needed something to wash away the bad taste of Murderess Row. I leant back in the chair, and closed my eyes.

'So go on then, genius. What have we got so far?'

He sucked in a deep breath. 'Ok... on the surface, an open and shut case. A woman... a beautiful one, admittedly... gets pissed out of her skull and shoots her husband dead in the Green Mill, in front of a whole host of witnesses.'

'Most of who scarpered, along with Scarface and his crew.'

'She murdered him with her own gun, which she claims never leaves the house. It's seen in her hand just after she shot him, but she can't remember doing it, only watching him drop dead in front of her. '

'Quaintly put, but yes.'

'Just recounting the facts, boss. Several people saw it happen, including you... but your eyes were on James, so you didn't actually see Daphne pull the trigger. In reality, it happened so fast, and so unexpectedly, that no one actually saw her do it.'

I sat up. Archie had a good point. *'No one saw her pull the trigger,'* I repeated.

'So did she?'

I leant back again, and threw my eyes to the ceiling. 'She must have done. Forensics proved it was the gun that shot him. We all saw it fall from her hand to the floor.'

'So it is an open-and-shut case then.'

My eyes fell back down, and focused on him staring intently at me. 'By the look, I take it you don't believe that?'

He went back to munching a few peanuts. 'I don't want to believe it, like you. We know she was set up, but how? And just as importantly, why?'

'It has to be something to do with whatever's in that safe deposit box. But it's looking less and less likely it's a fortune in cash... so what is it that everyone seems to want?'

'We know the mob fraternity is involved, James was Capone's bookkeeper. But Scarface wouldn't call on the likes of kids like Donnie and Nancy... he's got professionals for that kind of thing. Someone raided the white house, but I'm beginning to wonder if they were looking for *two* things, not one?'

Archie was cooking on gas, and boiling me up along with him. 'It's another good point. They probably broke in when our perfect couple were en route to the Green Mill, and tried and failed to find the key.'

'But easily found the other thing they needed... Daphne's Luger.'

'To incriminate her in the murder.' Suddenly, the cartoon light bulb was flashing a blue-coloured light. 'Nancy wasted no time making sure Daphne knew if she told her where *it* was, she would get off.'

136

'But they got it wrong. They assumed she would know where the safe deposit box key was hidden, but in fact she had no idea it even existed.'

'And when that failed, they made a last gasp attempt to find it in James's office, and ransacked that too.'

'Not knowing we'd already got it,' Archie grinned.

'Fat lot of use it is though, with Ebenezer Scrooge wielding an iron fist.'

'We need Daphne to visit the bank.'

'Which means we won't know what's in the box until, and if she's released.'

'Did you have to say that?'

Archie sat in silence, apart from the munching noises emanating from his brain food. I closed my eyes again, running through the latest but just as depressing barnstorming we'd done.

Between us we'd worked out why Daphne had been set up, and that the sting had failed. But it didn't help the gal herself, unless we could prove it to those outside our four walls.

We still didn't know what the deposit box contained, or what could possibly be so desirable to two rookie youngsters. We didn't know who the mysterious Mickey was.

And we sure as hell didn't know how they'd managed to make it look like Daphne was a cut-and-dried murderer.

Archie must have been thinking the same things. Suddenly the munching stopped. 'Sandie, we need another look at the crime scene.'

'Is that going to help?'

'Dunno. But I got me a feeling that's where the answer lies.'

I dragged myself to my weary feet. 'Well, my peanut-eating genius, there's no time like the present. It's not yet three, so the place shouldn't be rolling in punters for a while.'

'Can I bring my own nuts?'

Chapter 26

Tom looked like he was about to faint as we walked in. 'Hold me up... the honourable Sandie Shaw, *three* times in a week?'

'You complaining again, Tom?'

'Me? You drink my best produce for free, and don't tell me what's going on until someone gets murdered? What do I have to complain about?'

He didn't look as annoyed as his words would suggest, a slight smile on his lips. 'Stop moaning, Tom. You know you love me really.'

'Sure, my favourite gal. And this time you brought a date.'

I turned to Archie, wrapped an arm around his waist in an amused way. 'Well, Tom, he might need to stand on an orange box to kiss me, but he's all mine.'

Tom grinned, held out a hand to my date. 'Hey Archie, how you been?'

'Aw, y'know. My pain-in-the-ass boss keeps me in chains behind the desk, hidden so no one can see them.'

'You two know each other?'

Tom looked at me, raised his Mediterranean eyebrows. 'You didn't know?'

I narrowed my eyes at Archie. 'Hmm... I'm beginning to see there's a lot about my minion I don't know.'

He threw me his cheeky grin. 'Geez boss, a man-Friday has gotta keep a few a few secrets up his sleeve, see?'

'Maybe it's time I paid you more attention... or unshackled your chains a bit more often.'

He laid his head on my shoulder. 'Aw boss... you do need to let the kids go and have fun now and again.'

I saw his highly-amused, even cheekier grin, and took my arm swiftly from his waist. 'Just nibble your peanuts, and keep quiet like a good boy.'

Tom pulled out the real stuff, for the third time. 'So I guess this ain't a social call, Sandie.'

It wasn't a question, he already knew. 'My diminutive little bloodhound here, he wanted to sniff around the crime scene a bit, see if he could find a scent or two.'

'Good luck with that. At least someone cares more than the police department. But you and I both saw what went down, gal. You can't blame them for taking it as cut-and-dried.'

'Everyone from Devey down wants Daphne in the chair, Tom. But Frank... well, he has doubts. And so do we, after diving deeper into the dirty waters of it all. But his hands are tied, so he's kind of working unofficially with us, to discover the real truth. Which has come back to right here.'

He shook his head, like he didn't want to believe anyone cared so much. 'Hell guys, you got one steep hill to climb. But do your worst, if it helps.'

I turned to Archie. 'Ok bloodhound, get sniffing.'

He looked like his tongue was hanging out in anticipation. 'Sure thing, boss. But I wasn't here that night, so you need to fill me in with exactly where everyone was, and how it happened.'

I sat in the booth that had given me a view of everything that went down. Tom pulled the telephone from the back of the bar, and placed it on the top. 'I was standing here when the phone rang. Some guy asked to speak to James, so I called him over, and put the phone just where it is now. Then I served a couple of other punters, until...'

I filled in the rest of the blanks. 'I watched James as he answered the phone. I couldn't hear what he said, but from his lips it seemed like he said *"Hello?"* three or four times, then shook his head and put the receiver down. Just as he turned away, he spotted Daphne, and… well, you know the rest.'

Archie was pacing up and down like Sherlock Holmes, but with a bag of peanuts instead of a pipe. 'So Daphne had just come back into the bar, drunk as a skunk… and not alone?'

'My eyes were on James when the shots were fired. It was a few seconds later when I turned to look at Daphne. That Nancy was right behind her; they'd gone to the washroom together. A few other people were close to her, all staring in disbelief at what she'd done.'

Sherlock was looking thoughtful. 'So, the phone call, getting Daphne in the doorway… the fact no one actually saw her pull the trigger? I think you're right boss, it was all a setup.'

Tom was shaking his head rather a lot again, but Archie was confirming the darkest thoughts that had been spinning around my head for a day or two. 'The phone call was the way of getting James away from Capone, and closer to the door ready for when Daphne would walk back in. So she could take the rap for his murder, and then be willing to tell her female lover where the key was, in exchange for her freedom. Genius.'

Tom was still skeptical. 'That's all well and good, but we both saw the gun in her hand, right after the shots were fired. Then we all watched it drop to the floor. If it was a setup, how the hell did they get her to shoot the husband she loved?'

Archie was pacing again. 'Hmm… dastardly indeed. Such a task would seem impossible. Unless…'

'Archie... I mean, Sherlock? Are you getting carried away again?'

'Please Watson... sorry, boss... give me a minute to follow my nose.'

'As you wish, sir. Far be it from me to interrupt such brilliant detectivating.'

'Now you're just taking the piss.'

'Not my place to do such a thing, Holmes.'

He looked like he was about to retort, but then shook his head, and strode to the back of the room. Tom joined me in the booth. 'Your man is getting into the spirit,' he grinned.

'Yes, but don't do him down. He was the one whose sixth sense found the key no one else could find, and he helps me barnstorm when I can't put the pieces together.'

'Sounds like he's a valuable companion.'

I found my head nodding again. 'Yes, he is. Sometimes I don't know what I'd do without him and his irreverent attitude.'

'Sounds like a match made in private investigator heaven,' he grinned, and then looked around. 'Where's he gone, anyway?'

I looked around too. There was no sign of Archie. 'Who knows? Probably taking a pee. Or nipped back to replenish his peanuts.'

Tom laughed. 'You know the strange thing, Sandie? I anticipated a slowdown in trade after what went down, but the opposite has happened. Now I just have to put up with folks coming in so's I can show 'em the bloodstains on the floor. Which ain't there anymore anyway.'

'You should wipe a little tomato ketchup around, Tom. Satisfy their morbid curiosity. Seems nothing bring in the punters like a good murder.'

He threw his eyes to the ceiling. 'Sometimes I wonder if god has totally forsaken this place. Each and every day it feels more like hell on Earth.'

'That's one thing you don't need to tell me, Tom.'

Our conversation was interrupted, in a slightly unusual way. By a single shouted word.

'Bang!'

Chapter 27

A little shocked, we both turned to look in the direction of the shout. For a moment I could see nothing, but then I noticed two fingers pointing at me, like a child shaping the barrel of a gun.

A second later, Archie's grinning face appeared, from a somewhat unexpected place. Just his head, nothing else.

'*Archie!* I know you're the height of a ten year old, but you don't have to act like one.'

'Maybe not, boss. But you're gonna want to hear what I'm saying next.'

'I am?'

'Sure. I know how it was done.'

He stepped from behind the curtain at the back of the room. Not around it, *through* it. 'It's clever, I'll admit. Got me thinking hard for a minute.'

I glanced at Tom, whose head moved from side to side in wonder. Or amusement, one or the other. But seeing Archie, and just where he'd reappeared from, had started a chain reaction of thoughts. I knew what he was going to say before he said it.

He strode back to us, his fingers tapping his chin. 'It all makes sense now,' he said thoughtfully.

'Sherlock, you can stop making pretend guns with your fingers now.'

He glanced at his two fingers, and hastily separated them. 'Oh, yeah... sorry boss. But it was all made possible by the curtains, see?'

Tom still looked bemused. 'They've been there since the dawn of time. Always drawn back by ties at the entrance, but draping the whole of the back wall.'

'Ah yes... they look like one huge curtain each side, but they're not, are they?'

'Um, no. Six separate ones, but set to look like just one curtain on each side.

'Exactly! Step this way, I want to show you something.'

'Archie... no more Sherlock, ok?'

'Sure, boss,' he said as he led us to the entranceway. 'See, guys? Ok, you already know this, Tom, but look... the curtains aren't set right back to the rear wall. There's a foot or so of space.'

'How is that relevant?'

'Because someone could conceal themselves here, poke just the tip of the barrel through the joint in the curtains, and fire!'

Tom didn't look convinced. 'Ok, that's possible...'

'Likely.'

'Ok, likely, but it doesn't explain how we all saw the gun in Daphne's hand, a moment after she shot him.'

I filled in for Archie. 'That's because it *was* in her hand.'

'Huh?'

'Exactly!' a delighted Archie exclaimed. 'As I said, it all makes sense now.'

'Take the stage, Archie,' I said, already knowing how the play ended, but feeling he deserved the limelight.

'Daphne's own gun was stolen from her house, just after she'd left for here. Then somehow, it was handed to the perpetrator, who was already here before Capone arrived. The phone call ruse got James to the bar, just after the shooter went to the washroom at the same time Daphne did. He then hid behind the curtain until she got back. Then he fired.'

Tom's shaking head had turned into a nodding one. 'That's all feasible, but it doesn't explain how the gun ended up in Daphne's hand.'

I took over. 'That's the bit of the sting that could have gone wrong. The shooter was banking on all eyes being on James as he fell to the floor. It would have only taken him a couple of seconds to slip from the curtain, and reach Daphne who was only six feet away, standing there in utter shock.'

Archie finished off. 'She would hardly have been aware a gun had been pressed into her hand, which is why she dropped it a second or two later.'

'But by then the damage had been done. We all assumed she was the shooter, because the evidence was staring us in the face.'

'Geez.' It didn't seem like Tom could say any more words. But I could.

'Archie, you're a genius. You deserve another catering-size box of peanuts for that.'

Tom headed for the bar. 'He deserves another few shots of the real stuff. I think we all do.'

We sat in the booth together, discussing the revelations. Tom was still hesitant about one thing. 'Thinking about it though, the shooter took a risk hoping Daphne's fingers would actually curl around the gun, surely?'

'Not really. He only had a second to make it happen, but even if she hadn't taken hold if it, all he had to do was drop it on the floor, right underneath her arm. What would you have though if you'd heard the gun clatter to the floor?'

'Exactly the same as I thought anyway.'

'Like we all would have done. It was a bonus her reflex action was to grab hold of something placed in her hand.'

Tom sank his shot, and poured all of us another. 'So what happens now?'

'Ah... that's the rub. *We* now know how it was done, and almost the full story, but we can't actually prove it.'

'Not without a confession from Donnie or Nancy.'

'Or the mysterious Mickey... although I'm now thinking I saw him in here that night.'

Tom narrowed his eyes. 'Tell me.'

'There were three guys sitting drinking together before Capone arrived. You remember them, Tom?'

'Kinda. It's a bit unusual for three guys to be here without gals. But I could never pick them out of a line up.'

'Neither could I. To my regret, I didn't take much notice. They seemed innocent enough. But just when James answered the phone, I was vaguely aware of one of them headed to the John. It had got to be our man.'

'But you couldn't identity him either?'

My eyes threw themselves to the ceiling. '*Goddamn it*... I was too busy watching James. Not a chance of identifying him, not for certain.'

Tom slipped a hand on my arm. 'Hey gal, you had no reason to take any notice. Not until it was too late anyway.'

'Even if I could, it's not helping us now. We only have one hope left... get a confession out of the people we've already identified as being involved.'

'No problem then,' Archie grinned.

'Sure, like they're just gonna roll over and confess to being accessories to murder.'

My pseudo-Sherlock assistant was still grinning, as he finished his gin. 'Well, far be it from me to stick my pipe in again... but I might have a suggestion there.'

147

Chapter 28

'It'll never work.'

'Sure it will, with you around to back us up, Frank.'

He shook his head, not at all convinced. Archie added his two-cents-worth. 'Hey Frank, I can be very persuasive with a camera!'

'That's not the point. You don't know how they'll react, and I'm off-duty in a half-hour.'

'Does that matter, Frank? The perceived threat should be enough.'

'It's too dangerous... and risky, for me as well as you.'

Archie and me had headed straight to the precinct from the Green Mill. Sherlock's plan had more holes in it than a Swiss cheese, but I had to admit the small chance it had of success was scarily appealing.

Apart from that, it was the only chance we had of getting Daphne cleared.

We'd reached Frank's office just as the sun was disappearing behind the skyscrapers. He'd not exactly looked thrilled to find us there just as he was winding up for the day, but good man as he was, he'd heard us out.

And then shot us down.

'Don't you want to see justice done, Frank?' I said, as pitifully as I could manage.

He knew me too well to be fooled. 'Sure I do. But this isn't the way, Sandie.'

'So if you've got a better suggestion, we're all ears.'

'I... aw, geez. I'd say it again, but I run the risk of sounding like a broken record.'

'Consider it said. So are you with us?'

'Look, guys. I'll be off duty, so I can't legally make an arrest.'

'You might not have to. There's such a thing as a citizen's arrest, if we're stretching a point. And anyway, Donnie and Nancy won't know you're not on duty if you just happen to have forgotten to take your uniform off.'

'Talking of stretching a point, Sandie?'

'Ok, maybe so. But we'll need a couple of other officers along too.'

'You can't be serious?'

'If you saw Daphne's face, you'd know I am.'

He flailed his hands in the air, like it was a last-gasp defence. 'Ok, I know you're serious.' He walked to the window, and stood staring out like he was looking for some kind of divine intervention. It was likely the only thing that would get us out of his office without a result.

He knew just as well as we did it wasn't going to come. It had already been said that god had long since left Chicago.

He turned back to us. 'There's a couple of officers coming on shift soon, who ain't been corrupted yet, as far as I know. I could have a word in their ears.'

'That's the spirit, Frank.'

'Yeah, sure. This goes against every personal rule I possess, Sandie, and it also entails all of us breaking *actual* rules. You're asking a lot.'

'We're well aware of that, Frank. But we'll put in a good word for you if you end up in Cook County.'

He glared at me. 'Is that your attempt at humour?'

'Sorry. Me and my big mouth. It's not going to come to that, Frank. Not when you can take the credit for cracking a seemingly open-and-shut case. And if you'd seen Daphne's face...'

149

'Ok, ok... just quit with the emotional blackmail, please. We'll do it, even if it's my last act as a serving officer.'

'I told you, it won't come to that. You'll be the people's hero.'

'Forgive me if I take that with a pinch of salt. The food on this particular plate is way too raw, and there's only a slim chance it'll ever get cooked.'

I had to nod my agreement. 'Well aware of that. There's hardly much hope of us warming anything up, but it's still one chance we're prepared to take. And let's face it, it's the *only* chance.'

'Run me through what you want me to do.'

Nine in the evening, and Archie and me got organized in the office. I was dressed in what I assumed were suitable clothes for the role I was playing, and Sherlock looked every bit of what he was supposed to look like.

A long gabardine Ulster coat almost reached the floor. A jaunty, not too expensive Fedora hat stood proudly on his head, and the all-important camera and flashlight, borrowed from his news-photographer brother, sat on my desk ready for action.

The phone jangling away seemed to jar my nerves to shreds in the almost-silence. It was Frank, telling us he was just about to leave the office, on his way to pick us up in fifteen.

I told him we were ready, and not to sound so nervous. He laughed nervously, and killed the call.

Archie and me sank a final whisky, chinking the glasses to wish us both a successful sting. This whole murky affair had been all about a sting, and when Archie had told me of his plan, it felt strangely ironic.

We were about to create a sting, in order to disprove the original sting.

I just wished I could feel more confident about its success.

Chapter 29

We sat in Frank's car, parked in the side street where those picking up the dancers from the Chicago theatre waited. It was almost ten in the evening, and a light but very cold rain had begun to fall, Mother Nature's idea of a slightly sick joke.

Further down from us, out of sight of the marks we were waiting for, was a police car with Frank's two loyal officers inside. They were officially on duty, but an agitated Frank wasn't, even though he looked like he was, still dressed in his police uniform.

I hoped none of them would be needed, for the sake of Frank's career. He'd told the two officers he was working late, and needed them for a special operation, one which they had been left to assume was official.

If Donnie picked Nancy up from the stage door as we hoped, and Archie and me played the sting to perfection, all would be well. If it went south, and the crap hit the fan, Frank would be the one to suffer.

He knew that all too well, hence the wringing hands.

Around us, a few of the dancers were being escorted into the waiting cars. The show had finished. Still there was no sign of either Donnie or Nancy, but I knew from my rat-infested previous visit that she might be the last one out.

The possibility also existed she'd finally found the courage to dump him, and he wasn't there at all... but in their current uncertain situation, that would be unlikely. It wouldn't be a good move for either of them. Whether they liked it or not, they needed each other.

As the minutes passed, the doubts began to creep in. Maybe they'd finally had enough, and panicked. Cleared off, away from Chicago. Maybe neither of them was there at all.

I tried to convince myself that wasn't too likely either... as each day had passed, and with Daphne well incarcerated for the murder, they were probably thinking they'd got away with it.

If they were, they had a shock coming their way.

I still couldn't seem to stop thinking the worst though.

Suddenly, my thoughts were redundant. I'd just about convinced myself the lovebirds weren't going to show, when they appeared around the corner of the alley. We watched them walk quickly through the drizzle, arms around each other's waists.

Part one of the plan had come to pass.

'You know what you've got to do, Frank?' I said quietly.

'Sure,' he said back, wringing his hands even tighter together.

'Don't worry, we'll do our best to make sure you don't need to be involved.'

'Sure,' he said again.

I nodded to Archie, and we slipped out of the car, and followed our marks. The night air was one step off freezing, the drizzle one step below that. I wrapped my scarf around my neck, trying to ward off the tiniest of snowflakes.

The youngsters a hundred yards in front of us never looked back as they headed for Nancy's apartment. It was a kind of comforting sign... they clearly didn't feel the need to check they weren't being followed.

Of course it could have been they were just too naively stupid, thinking they'd got away with their roles in the sting. If they were, they were about to get a rude awakening.

153

Hardly anyone was around as they reached the street where Nancy's tenement block was situated. Archie and me quickened our step. We were just fifty yards behind them as they climbed the three steps to the outside door of the block.

This time there didn't seem to be any hesitation on Nancy's part. No goodnight kiss, no slap in Donnie's face. The key was placed straight into the lock. They were clearly intending to spend the night together.

If Archie and me played our parts well, it might not be in the building they intended.

I took a quick glance around. No one else seemed to be in sight, the block situated in a part of town it wasn't really advisable to be walking about after nine at night.

I nodded to Archie, who raised his camera. We only had a few seconds before they disappeared through the door, into an unknown apartment, which could be one of rather a lot.

As we made the foot of the steps, I called out sharply. *'Nancy Pelowski, isn't it?'*

They both turned, a little surprised someone had spoken. Nancy looked nervous, but growled out the words anyway. 'Who wants to... oh, geez, it's you...'

Archie halted the conversation. It was a bit hard for anyone to speak, as the little world of the doorway lit up like daylight.

He took their photo, and then looked at me and grinned. 'Got it, boss.'

Chapter 30

Donnie had never seen me. Nancy had, but she had no idea who I actually was. As they both shielded their faces, a moment too late, I took great delight in introducing myself. Kind of.

'Hello, you two. I'm Mary Moonshine, investigative reported for the *Tribune*. This is my photographer, Arthur Warburton.'

Archie grinned. 'Pleased to make your acquaintance.'

He might have been pleased. Neither of the lovebirds seemed to be. Nancy wasn't too keen on us being there. 'Get lost. Leave us alone.'

Donnie seemed to agree. *'Go to hell,'* he cried.

I wasn't going to go to hell. I'd already been there, not so long ago. 'We just need a word, you two. In private, yeah?'

That seemed to be the last straw for Donnie. He excused himself, taking his girlfriend by surprise. Looking like he didn't know where to put himself, he stuttered his excuses. 'Listen, baby. I gotta be somewhere, ok. You talk to these reporters, yeah? I'll... I'll catch you tomorrow...'

Nancy wasn't having any of it, once she got the power of speech back. *'Really?* You running out on me, you sniveling length of sewer pipe? Go on then, coward. Show your true colours and beat it...'

'Hey, I said I gotta...'

He realized he was standing on swamp ground, so the words dried up. Suddenly he was all action, turning on his heels and brushing past us, on his way to be somewhere. Archie wasn't having any of that either. Donnie had only got ten feet when he called after him.

'Um... Mr. Caravello, I wouldn't do that if I were you...'

He turned to look back at us. *'You threatening me, you little weasel?'*

'Not exactly. But you should maybe know, my boss here has got the go-ahead for a front-page scoop on what's gone down lately... and I've got a lovely picture of the two of you to go with it. So you might want to stick around, see what she has to say?'

'You...' Donny didn't seem able to find a suitable expletive, but Nancy didn't give him much chance anyway. 'Just get your chicken legs in here, Donnie... if you know what's good for you.'

I wasn't sure if Nancy was referring to the threat from Archie and me or the threat from a woman scorned, but it had the desired effect. Donnie huffed and puffed his teenage way back to the doorway, Nancy turned the key, and we filed inside.

The apartment was much as I expected the pad of a chorus dancer to look. Roughly the same size as mine, the sparsely-furnished living area included a tiny basic kitchen against one wall, and two doors leading off the room. It was a fair bet one led to a single bedroom, one to the bathroom.

Both of them looked like entertaining visitors was the last thing they expected to be doing, their furtive eyes flicking around the space like they anticipated more of us would be waiting there. Donnie slumped onto the threadbare couch, his eyes giving away the fact he was feeling like he'd been caught in the proverbial spider's web. Nancy stood on the far side of the room, watching us both like a praying mantis.

She was the first to speak. 'So why the interest in two simple folks like us, hey?'

156

I tried to smile sweetly. 'Because you two were instrumental in setting up Daphne deMountford.'

Donnie sneered. 'Who the hell is she?'

'Oh, my sources tell me that you and your girlfriend know her very, very well.'

Something clicked in Nancy's head. 'Say, you were at the Mill that night, when she shot her husband, weren't you?'

'Sure I was... but I'm surprised you had the time to clock me, after you disappeared once you'd done what you needed to.'

'I don't know what you mean.'

Archie, prowling around the room, suddenly lit it up with another blinding flash. That didn't seem to go down too well either.

'Can't you tell your monkey to stop doing that?' Donnie growled, rubbing his eyes.

'Monkey? Arthur here is one of the best photographers in the business. And he likes to make sure there'll be plenty of shots of you two to choose from. You know, so we can select the one that leaves no one in any doubt *who you are*.'

Donnie glanced to Nancy. She gave him a look of thunder, and spat out the words. 'You and your scheming, you lousy slimeball.'

'Hey, shut your mouth, Nanc. They don't know nothing.'

'Oh, but we do, Donnie. We know exactly how you make it look like Daphne was the shooter... and that it was in fact *you* who shot James.'

He flew to his feet. 'Say, I didn't kill no one, ok?'

Another blinding flash from Archie's camera, and he sat down quickly again, covering his eyes. *'Will you stop him doing that?'*

'Sorry, he has an obsession with snapping criminals. You might just have to put up with it, amongst other things.' I

157

glanced back to the blank notebook in my hand. 'So if you didn't kill James, then who did? Mickey?'

Nancy turned away, her eyes glossed over. *'Geez,'* she breathed.

Donnie had a few more words to say. *'How the hell..?'*

'We have our sources. So we know that you worked for James occasionally, and somehow found out about the key.'

He buried his face in his hands. 'What do you want from us?'

'The truth. Oh, and just so you know, the police are on their way, so don't think about trying anything.'

Nancy finally moved. 'I need to go take a leak... if that's ok?'

I didn't see any reason why not. She was likely one step away from peeing herself anyway. I waved to say it was ok, and she hurried through the bathroom door, closing it behind her. Archie's camera flashed again, and Donnie retorted again. 'For the love of god... you gonna get him to snap her on the loo too?'

Archie grinned. 'Can I?'

'Maybe give it a rest for now, Arthur? Donnie has a few things he wants to tell us, haven't you, Donnie?'

'Sure. Might as well tell you everything.'

His sudden cave-in took me a little by surprise. Ok, we'd got him over a barrel, but it looked like he was crumpling a bit easier than I'd expected. Even when his hand crept towards his jacket pocket I still hadn't tuned in.

It was only the next second when everything got as clear as day.

He leapt to his feet, a revolver in his shaking hands. 'You... you stupid broad. You think the likes of me is gonna cave in to reporters? You better thing again, old woman...'

158

Now he'd insulted me, just like his girlfriend had. I felt like throwing a sharp object in his direction, but my hands were kinda tied. It would never reach him before the gun went off, the bullet heading inevitably in my direction. His eyes were wild, flicking around the room like a cornered gazelle's. He wouldn't normally have the weird kind of guts it took to kill someone, but right then he was all out of options.

And in that kind of scenario, the abnormal could easily happen.

'Into the bedroom, both of you. And give me that camera,' he snarled.

Archie glanced to me. I nodded sadly. A teenager getting one over on me with a gun in his hand also wouldn't look good on my resume, but there was no sensible option other than to comply.

Archie shook his head, and held the camera out for him to take. 'Sure, Donnie. Whatever you say.'

Chapter 31

Donnie was looking right at the camera as he reached out to grab it. Archie took full advantage. Another blinding flash, and the gun-wielding thug was blinded. This time I was fully tuned into my photographer's intentions, and one second later the gun was wrenched out of his hand, and into mine instead.

Donnie fell back to the couch. 'Geez, I told you to stop him doing that...' he whimpered.

I pointed the gun at him. 'And you need to know the camera is more powerful than the gun. *Now* can we talk?'

'Guess I don't have a choice, lady.'

At least he didn't call me *old woman*. But he hadn't finished trying to get one over on us, and sneered like he'd won a minor victory. 'At least Nanc got away.'

I looked at Archie, who ran to the bathroom door, and hammered on it. There was no reply. Donnie laughed. 'She ain't there, flash man. Fire escape is accessed through the bathroom window.'

'Aw hell,' Archie exclaimed, and then turned back to Donnie and grinned. 'At least she won't get very far.'

'Wh... what do you mean?'

I shot him down. 'I told you the police were on their way. Maybe I under-exaggerated.'

'You... you're kidding me.'

He didn't sound very sure. Then, a knock on the door made certain of what was what. Frank's voice, from the other side. *'Chicago Police Department. Open up.'*

Archie opened up. A slightly-relieved Frank was standing there, with the two other officers. They each had a firm grip on a flustered-looking Nancy's arms.

'You still think I'm kidding?' I couldn't help saying.

Frank and the others walked into the room. He saw the gun in my hand. 'Better let me take that,' he said, holding his arm out.

Donnie, clearly a quick thinker, made the most. '*She tried to kill me...*'he cried.

'Sure she did, Donnie.'

'That's his gun, Frank. He pulled it on us, until my trusty cameraman blinded him.'

He grinned, the moment easy to imagine. Then he turned to the other two officers. 'You two, wait outside, make sure no one else tries to come in.'

They nodded and left, closing the door behind them. Frank shook his head. I said the only thing I could. 'Sorry, Frank. Good job we stationed someone at the bottom of the fire escape... although I had no idea it was accessed from the bathroom.'

'Same end result. At least I'm here now, to hear their confession for myself. *Aren't I, you two?*'

They both looked at the three of us, like they knew their dreams of a life in Florida had totally unraveled. Even so, Donnie couldn't help another dig.

'Just tell that little shrimp to keep his camera away from me.'

Nancy sat on the other end of the couch, as far away from Donnie as she could get. Her legs were likely not able to keep her upright anymore. I sat in the single chair, Archie and Frank stood looking down on the two youngsters. Frank laid out his store.

'Ok you two, you need to know we are aware of what went down that night. So the game is up, and telling more lies is just going to make things worse. Are you hearing me?'

Nancy nodded silently. Donnie growled out the words. 'I'm blinded, not deaf, see?'

I needed to twist the knife, and help the confession on its way. 'Frank, I believe Donnie here is the shooter.' I didn't believe it, but there's nothing like getting a confession for lesser crimes by accusing someone of a more serious one. It seemed to have the desired effect.

'Say, I told you, lady... it wasn't me.'

Frank knew what I was doing. 'Maybe, but if you tell me who was the shooter, I might try and believe you.'

He buried his face in shaking hands. 'It was Mickey. It was all his idea.'

'Mickey who?'

He laughed cynically.' Yeah, sure. I'm gonna go down for collusion, but if I tell you who Mickey is, I ain't gonna last a week in Cook County, you get me?'

Frank glanced at his co-conspirator. 'Nancy?'

'Hey, I don't have no clue who he is, but even if I did I wouldn't tell you. Donnie deserves to get slashed, but I don't.'

'Hey, baby...'

'Don't call me *baby*... ever again. I never liked it anyway.'

I knew Frank wasn't going to get anywhere with that line of enquiry. It wasn't really why Archie and me were in investigative reporter mode anyway. 'Maybe leave that for the holding cell, hey Frank?'

He nodded. 'Ok, tell me what went down, in your own words, right from the beginning.'

Donnie let out a deep, resigned sigh. 'Ok. Sometimes I did a bit of work for James, see? One day I saw him with a necklace, a big blue diamond right in the middle of it...

'That's some piece of kit, James.'

162

'It's for Daphne's birthday. And trust me, Donald, when you've got someone like her as your wife, it's worth twice its weight in gold.'

'You better keep it safe until the day then.'

'Oh, I intend to, somewhere she won't find it.'

'So he decided to put it in a safe deposit box?'

'Yeah. One evening I followed him, saw him go into the Wallace and Simpson bank. So I knew where it was, but I couldn't find the key in his office.'

'You decided stealing it was a good idea then?'

'Sure. I roped Nancy in, to get... friendly with him, see if she could find out where it was. I told my mate too, and when Nanc got nowhere with James, he came up with the plan. He decided if they had a safe deposit box, his wife had to know where James kept the key.'

'This was Mickey, I take it?'

Donnie nodded silently. But something he said wasn't sitting easily. I glared at Nancy. 'So you made a play for James *before* Daphne?'

She grinned, like she really wanted to tell me the worst. 'Sure, and the English snob was well up for it. He was pretty damn good between the sheets as well.'

Donnie looked like it was news to him too. 'Say bab... Nanc... you never told me you got that far...'

'Just shut your mouth, mister nobody. It's for me to know how far I got.'

I shook my head to myself. Nancy might have been doing a Roxie Hart and shoving a vengeful lie down our throats... but then again maybe she wasn't. It could just have been I didn't do my job thoroughly enough. James had obviously kicked her into touch, but not before he actually might have been unfaithful.

Whichever way, there was no way to ever know for sure. Not now.

Frank shook his head, realizing he wasn't going to be told who Mickey was. 'So this plan... what did it entail?'

'I thought you guys had worked it out?'

'Just tell me, in your words.'

'Just tell him, Donnie. It's too late now.' Nancy looked desolate, like she'd finally given up.

Donnie's eyes glossed over. He was giving up too. 'Mickey, he's like, a bit on the edge... he came up with a plan to give Daphne no choice but to tell us. I didn't like it, but Mickey... he's got connections, see? I didn't have no choice.'

'Well, you did have a choice, Donnie.'

'You don't know Mickey. He's off his head most of the time.'

I glanced to Nancy. 'And what did *you* think, Nancy?'

She shook her head. 'It was a crazy plan. But that loudmouth sitting there told me the necklace was worth a fortune, and that we'd be heading off to a new life in Florida after I'd done my stuff. Me, I convinced myself to believe him. We all do one stupid thing in our lives, right?'

'Yeah, we all do,' I said, thinking that for most people it was a hell of a lot more than one thing. 'So, you decided to go along with it then?'

'Sure, for my sins. Quite a few sins, as it turns out.'

Chapter 32

'Go on, tell me the worst.'

'I got... friendly with Daphne, thought maybe she would let slip where the key was. I didn't have much luck, so we put the next bit of the plan into action. We didn't have much time, see? Her birthday was coming up. Mickey's plan was to give her no choice but to tell us.'

Frank looked disgusted. 'So you set up the sting at the Green Mill.'

Nancy glanced to Donnie like she hated him. 'Your turn, lowlife.'

He looked at her, but then shook his head, knowing he'd lost what little he had, including his girlfriend. 'I told Mickey it was a bad idea, that it would never work, but he wouldn't listen.'

'But it did work, didn't it?'

'Yeah, somehow. Nanc got Daphne drunk that night, to make sure she was so out of it she didn't know what was going on. Mickey was already there, with two of his mates.'

I cursed myself. I'd seen the guy, but not paid him enough attention. I told myself I was getting too old for the game I was in... maybe I *was* the old woman the kids seemed to think I was. Donnie, maybe fortunately, didn't give me anymore time to dwell on it.

'First I went to their place, searched for Daphne's gun. And tried to find the key too, so I could make it so Mickey's plan didn't have to go down. I found the gun, but not the key, so I had to carry on.'

'You telephoned the Mill, at an appointed time?'

'Yeah. Mickey made as if to leave, knowing Capone's men wouldn't let him get further than the outside door. I was already outside, making like I wanted to get in. While we was all arguing, I slipped Mickey the gun. Then I went to the phone booth on the other side of North Broadway, and made the call. Mickey needed to be sure James was close to the back of the room, so he could get a good shot. He hid himself...'

'Behind the rear curtain.'

'You know?'

'I told you, we know everything.'

'Nanc made sure Daphne was back from the washroom at the right time. Mickey did the deed, and then shoved the gun into her hand.'

Frank shook his head. 'And the rest is history. A kind of history anyway.'

'I told you, I didn't want to do it. It was all for nothing anyway.' He pointed a shaky finger at me. '*She* turned up at the cell block, just as Daphne was about to tell Nanc where the key was.'

I shook my head, in a vaguely-satisfied kind of way. 'What you two don't know is that it really was all for nothing. Daphne had no idea a safe deposit box even existed, let alone where the key was.'

'*What?*' they both cried together.

Archie rammed the point home. 'Yeah. So you got yourselves jail time for absolutely nothing. Not your best day, huh?'

Nancy let out a desolate-sounding wail. Dreams of a Florida beach had long gone, but images of a jail cell were quickly taking their place. At the end of the day she'd done less wrong than any of them, but she was still complicit in framing someone for murder. Her sentence wouldn't be short, Roxie Hart lookalike or not.

Frank pulled out a set of handcuffs. 'Donnie Caravello, I'm arresting you for your part in attempting to mislead the Chicago police into wrongful arrest. And for breaking and entering, twice… and maybe a few other misdemeanors that might come to light.'

He finally took his hands from his face. 'Do I get a shorter sentence for pleading guilty?'

'That's up to the judge. It might help if you told us Mickey's full name.'

He laughed cynically. Yeah, sure. More than my life's worth. Really, it is.'

'Yeah, I thought as much.' Frank opened the door, and called in the other two officers. 'These two need to be carted to the holding cells. I'll take their official statements in the morning.'

He handcuffed Donnie. One of the others did the same to Nancy. Both of them pierced angry stares into me as they were led away.

For some reason they seemed to blame me for their crimes. For a moment, I really wished I was Mary Moonshine, with a front page scoop waiting, and a couple of revealing photographs to go with it.

Frank looked like a weight had been lifted off his shoulders. Despite the fact he'd pretended to be on duty when he wasn't, the end result had justified the means. When he interviewed the perpetrators in the morning, and took their official written confessions, his unofficial actions would be vindicated.

Devey wouldn't be too pleased at first, until the newspapers praised the police department for their sterling work, at which point he would be only too happy to take the credit.

167

Frank was unlikely to get any. But he wouldn't lose his pension either.

He held out a hand to Archie and me. 'Well done, you two. Really couldn't have done this without you. Didn't think this evening would work, but I guess you know kids better than I do.'

I smiled to myself. That was a debatable point. But what mattered had been achieved. In a few hours, the two people who had set Daphne up for the fall would be the ones to also set her free.

That shone a ray of sunshine over everything else. The mysterious Mickey would remain mysterious, that much I knew. Donnie and Nancy were far too scared for their lives to ever give him up.

For them, it was likely a wise decision. It didn't change the fact the man behind the genius plan might have seen it fail, but he'd also got away with it.

Somehow I knew that, despite my aversion to the mob, our paths would cross again... sooner or later.

As Frank drove us home, I found a smile for Archie. 'Well played, you. Brilliant and inventive use of a camera. Seems you saved the day, yet again.'

Even in the dark, I could feel him going red. 'Aw boss... all in a day's work, y'know. I might even get a hug from Daphne.'

'I was going to give you a cash bonus, but if a hug is all you want...'

He shook his head. 'Well... hugs from beautiful Amazonian women can only go so far... if you see what I mean.'

168

Chapter 33

A watery sun was just dipping below the skyline of Chicago when I received a phone call. Frank's words brought a huge smile to my face.

'I have Daphne's release papers in my hand. I'm just going off-duty, so I thought the least I could do was pick her up from Cook County. I guess you'll want to accompany me?'

He didn't need to ask. 'Our ex-lovebirds did the necessary then?'

'Sang like a couple of bluebirds... everything except who Mickey is, of course.'

'No surprise there. We'll never get him that easily.'

'For sure. We're going over known felons with that first name now, but no one looks hopeful.'

'Right now it doesn't matter. Getting Daphne out of that hellhole does. I'll be waiting.'

I made Archie's day when I gave him the news. The cheeky smile was as big as I'd ever seen it. He asked if he could come too, but I said no. Somehow I knew Daphne wouldn't be in the best frame of mind, released or not. She would need a day or so to get her head around not having to face the chair.

The less people who were with her while she did, the better.

I sent Archie home, and promised we'd all meet up the next day.

Frank had telephoned the jail ahead of us getting there, but we still had to hang around until they released Daphne. Somehow an inmate of Murderess Row being freed without a sleazy lawyer pulling strings seemed to be extremely unusual.

Frank had put his neck on the line again, authorizing the release papers before Devey and his cronies had given him the nod, but he knew they had little choice. He'd been told in writing who the murderer was, and in Frank's heart that meant the innocent had to go free, even though the real perpetrator remained at large.

It was a full half-hour before the door to reception opened, and the matron appeared with a quiet and subdued Daphne by her side. Her eyes looked blank, like she couldn't believe she was a free woman. Irene Morston however, wasn't so silent.

'I don't know how you pulled it off, but just get her out of my sight, ok? I got other so-called innocent victims to take care of.'

I gave her a stony glare, but Frank put a hand on my arm, and stopped me from saying what I really wanted to. At the end of the day the two-faced matron was losing an inmate she saw as a lucrative captive, so wasn't as pleased by developments as the rest of us.

I watched her disappear through the door, and then turned to Daphne. She fell against me, tears rolling down her perfect cheekbones. *'How?'* she sobbed.

'Let's just say we got a confession from two people who knew you very well, and how to manipulate you. We need to get you home.'

I didn't tell her where home actually was right then. Going back to the white house wasn't an option. Apart from the fact everything that could be salvaged had been removed, someone who knew where she lived was still on the loose. It was a fair bet Mickey had given up on his plans, but there was no way to know for sure. Mobsters didn't like failure.

When it came down to it, Daphne didn't have a truly safe haven right then. There was only one place that even came close.

I wrapped my hand around hers as we sat together in the back of Frank's car. Still she'd only said one word, and looked like she was somewhere on another world. She was back in the very unsuitable dress she'd worn on the awful night, and even the most loose-fitting of my clothes wouldn't fit her. It wouldn't be the right thing anyway.

'Frank, I know this is taking up your downtime, but can we call at the precinct? Daphne's clothes are boxed up in the basement, and she can't go on wearing this dress… it isn't pleasing my nostrils.'

He nodded and smiled. 'How are you feeling, Daphne?'

'Grateful,' she mumbled. 'I don't know what else to feel right now. I can't get my head around what's happening to me.'

My heart missed a beat again. She looked a pitiful sight, and it wasn't sitting easily with me. Despite the niggling doubt in one part of my head, another part of it had believed she'd pulled the trigger. I seriously disliked myself for that. Now I had to do all I could to make it up to her… and to myself. It wasn't too clear which of us was in more need of tender loving care, from the point of view of regrets at least.

I tried to reassure her. 'Just for tonight you're coming back with me, once we've found you a few better clothes. If that's ok?'

She nodded silently, but I felt my hand squeezed a little tighter.

171

Frank dropped us off at the lobby door, and asked me to call him in the morning. I grabbed the box of clothes we'd extracted from the precinct basement, and led a still-subdued Daphne up the wooden stairs.

It was only as we walked into the apartment and closed the door behind us, that she burst into the floods of tears she'd been holding back. Somehow, seeing the apartment of a free woman had suddenly rammed everything home... quite literally.

I held her tight, let her see it through. There were no real words of comfort. She'd been through a week of hell, and in some ways it was over, but in others it would never be. She'd lost the man she loved, and no amount of time could ever change that.

There was just enough whisky left in the bottle to pour us a glass each. We both needed it, likely as much as each other. While we sipped the nectar I boiled up as much water as I could, and then packed her off for a bath, while I unpacked the box of clothes and laid them out on my bed.

A little while later she reappeared, wrapped in a big white bath towel. 'Feeling any better now?' I asked her.

I saw a slight smile. 'Yes, thank you. It feels like I've washed away some of the grime.'

'That's the spirit. I'm afraid I only have one bedroom, but you can take this bed. I'll sleep on the couch.'

She shook her head. 'It is a double bed. There is room for two, surely?'

'Daphne?'

She put a hand on my arm. 'Don't worry, my brief dalliance with the female sex is well and truly over. And I am from Ghana, Sandie. There, sleeping in the same bed is considered normal, whether or not you are in a sexual relationship. Please, do not make do with the couch.'

I smiled, slightly relieved. 'That goddamn thing isn't that comfortable anyway.'

Midnight wasn't too far away. I'd made sure the box of clothes included something for Daphne to sleep in, and a half-hour after the bath we found ourselves side-by-side in my bed. Somehow, it didn't feel that weird. Daphne was looking more like herself, but I noticed the occasional shudder rack her body, no doubt as a sudden recall of what she'd been through in the last few days stabbed a sword of reminder into her.

She looked like she was already three parts asleep, but as we exchanged a few last words, I could see the little wisps of steam coming out of her ears. Her fighting spirit was coming back, and a certain someone was helping with that.

Just before we turned out the bedside light, she said something quietly, and more determinedly that I'd ever heard her say anything before.

'We need to sleep now, Sandie. Tomorrow is the first day of the rest of our lives, and we have one task above all others.'

'We have?'

'Yes. No matter how long it takes, we must find the man who killed my husband.'

Chapter 34

The first day of the rest of our lives dawned bright and sunny. Whether it was some kind of sign from above or pure coincidence, there was no way to know.

It was still good to see though.

While we grabbed a little breakfast, I brought Daphne up to speed with everything that had happened in the last day or so, including the role Archie played in her salvation.

'Your little assistant needs my heartfelt thanks, I think,' she said.

'He's a diamond. He's been with me two years, but I'm just beginning to see how valuable he truly is.'

She smiled. 'And how valuable he will be in the future, no doubt.'

I looked her over. Dressed in a pair of black slacks, and a tight-fitting bobbled white jumper, she looked much more like the woman it was becoming clear she was. A new, determined look was easy to see in her dark eyes, and her hair was neatly brushed, and framing the flawless skin that hadn't looked flawless for a few days. Then, her next words confirmed she was back to her spirited self.

'I think first we need to retrieve my car, Sandie, before anyone steals it.'

The obvious point seared into my thoughts. 'Daphne, do you not think it's a bit too soon? The house...'

She shook her head. 'African women are resilient. I cannot change what has happened, but now I need to make sure it doesn't get any worse. The house, beautiful though it is, was never ours to own. But the car is, and we may need it from now on. I cannot abide public transport, anyway.'

One word she'd said didn't go unnoticed. *'We?'*

Her head lowered. 'You and Archie are the only true friends I have right now, apart from Frank of course. I am hoping we can try and find this Mickey together. You tell me Archie found the contents of the safe, so I have money to pay you.'

I cringed inside. Getting paid to bring about justice for a friend didn't seem right, not in this case. 'Let's just see, yeah? You might need that money for other things.'

She smiled, the dazzle returning. 'Thank you.'

'Ok, but there's something else we have to do, as it seems you're up to it. We need to visit the Wallace and Simpson bank.'

We headed downstairs to the office. Archie was already there. He let out a big beaming smile as he saw us. '*Daphne*... so good...'

The smile got wiped from his face. Daphne didn't hesitate, walked right up to him and kissed him. Full on, for a full five seconds, taking him and me totally by surprise.

As he staggered back, his eyes wide with shock as he grabbed the desk for support, he managed to gasp out the words. Amazingly.

'*Wh... what was that for?*'

Daphne smiled affectionately at his beetroot face. 'Sandie tells me it was your genius brain that was predominant in me being brought back to freedom. That was the least I could do. Thank you, Archie. So much.'

I couldn't help grinning at his shocked demeanor. What Daphne had done would stay with him for the rest of his life, that much I already knew. He pulled himself together, and swallowed hard. 'Aw... all in a day's work, y'know...'

175

'Yes, for which you are seriously underpaid. I must have a word with your boss about that, but right now we have things to do. We will see you later, my dear friend.'

We stood together on the sidewalk, gazing at the white house that didn't look any different from the road. Despite Daphne's determination, I saw the hesitation in her expression.

'We don't have to go inside, if it's too much.'

I saw a slight nod of the head. 'Perhaps I have convinced myself I am braver than I am.'

'Quite honestly, I don't think I would have the guts, after what...'

She stepped through the gate, and then turned to me and smiled. 'You are right, as usual. Perhaps we will just retrieve the car, and then never look back.'

'It might be for the best. All of your possessions are back at the station, except for the furniture.'

'The house was furnished when we rented it. So that is not an issue.'

'Then there is no need to go inside and risk upsetting you further. Let's just grab the car, and say goodbye?'

She nodded, and strode off around the side of the house towards the garage. She wasn't hanging around, and I knew why. She had a strong spirit, but after what had happened, neither the spirit nor her belonged at the white house anymore.

Suddenly, she needed to leave it behind as quickly as possible.

As we walked into the Wallace and Simpson bank, I spotted the Dickensian manager at the back of the teller's counter. He spotted us too, and for a moment looked a little

176

like a frightened mouse. Then he seemed to recover his prim and proper demeanor, and came out to greet us.

'Ah, so you're back. And this time with..?'

An elegant hand held out to him. 'Daphne deMountford. I trust there will be no problem with accessing *our* safe deposit box now?'

'Um... please give me a moment.' He disappeared again, into his office. Daphne looked curiously at me. 'He seems unsettled by our presence, or is that just my imagination?'

'No, it's not your imagination. Then again he belongs in the early Victorian era, so your statuesque black appearance likely displeases him.'

'Hmm... perhaps I should threaten him with my spear.'

She didn't have time to go get her spear. The manager was back, a sudden and totally false smile on his face, after he'd obviously checked the photograph in the file. 'I take it you have the key, madam?'

'Of course.'

He led us down a set of steps, and over to a thick vault door. His fumbling hands found the door key, and then he tapped in the code, spun the wheel, and the circular door swung slowly aside. He led us inside, to where three walls of the small room were lined with safe deposit boxes of various sizes. He didn't seem to want to leave.

'Would you like me to open it for you?' he said.

'We can manage from here, thank you.'

'But...'

I pointed him at the door. 'Please wait outside. Amazingly enough, women are quite capable of unlocking things.'

'*There's no need for that kind of attitude...*' he muttered, as I made sure he left the room.

177

I shook my head as I turned back to Daphne. 'Charles Dickens has a lot to answer for.'

'Indeed.' Suddenly she was looking pensive again. The key was in her hand, and she already knew what was inside the box. 'You know the crazy thing, Sandie?' she said, almost a whisper. 'James told me he'd got me a gift for my birthday, but he also said it wasn't as expensive as it looked, because we needed the money to spend on the beach house. The necklace that got him killed won't be that valuable. He only put it here so I wouldn't find it.'

'Oh Daphne...' My heart went out to the poor woman again. 'When is your birthday?'

'Today.'

'Hell.' It was yet another final straw for us both, when I'd believed there couldn't be any more final straws. I could feel the pain and the needless loss in my heart, and it was trying to break me just as much as it was her.

On her birthday, she was going through a thumping reminder that she'd lost the man she loved, and done so because a teenager got the wrong idea about how valuable her gift was.

It was a heartbreaker for sure.

'Would you like me to open the box?'

I could see the gloss of tears in her eyes. A shaking hand gave me the key. 'Yes please, if you would.'

I slipped the key into the lock of one of the slim boxes. As I did so, the thought occurred to me that it was a bit strange James had taken out a safe deposit box just to hide something of little real value. Maybe it was worth more than he was making out to his wife?

We were about to find out if it was strange or not. I slid the box out, and placed it on the table in the centre of the room. Daphne let out a little sob as her eyes fell on the

178

necklace. It was beautiful for sure, but it couldn't have been real. The blue diamond in its centre was huge, the kind of carats only the richest of industrialists and sheiks could afford.

James could never have pretended it was real, because it was so obviously fake. He would never have tried to, simply wanting his wife to have something that, like her, would turn heads. But Donnie's words in Nancy's apartment suddenly made sense. Being *"worth twice its weight in gold"* wasn't referring to the necklace itself, but to the fact he knew his wife would love and appreciate it.

In terms of the sting, it was for sure the final, tragic straw. James really had been killed for nothing.

Daphne held it in her hands, a smile on her face. And yet along with that, her eyes were full of tears. 'You need to consider that as your most precious possession, Daphne,' I said, the words forcing their way through the lump in my throat.

She nodded. I can do no other. James died for it, didn't he?'

It was a question there was no need to answer, but as I glanced back to the box, what I saw took any words away that I might have said. The necklace wasn't the only item in the box. I lifted out the well-worn book, and looked up to Daphne with a frown on my brow.

'I've got an awful feeling this is the real reason James owns this box,' I whispered.

Chapter 35

We left the bank as quickly as we could, both the necklace and the mysterious book hidden in Daphne's reticule. The manager still looked like a frightened mouse as we left, but as we hightailed it from the premises, he wasn't the only one.

I had a feeling the book in our possession was a hell of a lot more valuable than the necklace.

Daphne asked the all-important question. 'What do you think it is that's valuable enough to keep in a safe deposit box?'

'I only had a very quick flick through as you know, but it seems to be some kind of ledger, full of figures and notes which might be of serious interest to someone.'

She was on my wavelength straightaway. 'Like the taxman?'

'Yeah. And to a certain someone else, who doesn't want the taxman to see it.'

She shook her head, but her eyes clouded with fear. 'Do you think we're the only ones who know about it?'

Once again, there was no point in lying. 'That bank manager was looking shifty. There's a possibility that when I tried to pretend I was you to get access to the box, it aroused his suspicions. He might have known, and if he's in Capone's pocket, then who else knows?'

She shook her head slowly. 'You are making me fearful, Sandie.'

We reached home, said a brief hello to Archie, and then disappeared into the office. I needed to have a proper look through the contents of the ledger, and see just how fearful Daphne needed to be.

And anyone else who now possessed it.

We sat together behind the desk, and scanned through the pages. We didn't need to go as far as a detailed read; within the first few pages it was obvious just how frightened we needed to be.

James had said the necklace was metaphorically worth twice its weight in gold... the secret ledger was worth a hundred times that.

My voice seemed to want to whisper, even though no one could hear us. 'It's a record of Capone's dealings... every illegal transaction, names, dates. And a list of his known associates, and what role they played, going right back to his New York days.'

Daphne looked scared to death, realizing we were holding the hottest possession in Chicago. 'But why? Why would James do such a thing? Capone paid him well, seemed to think highly of him.'

'This is a mob boss we're talking about, Daphne. And he didn't get where he is by chance. One false move and James would be no more. Maybe he felt he needed some kind of insurance policy?'

'Or perhaps he was planning to go to the authorities with undeniable evidence? James wasn't comfortable working for who he was. He said to me a few months ago Capone was getting too big for his boots.'

I closed the ledger and looked at her with helpless eyes. 'There's no way we will ever know for sure now. But one thing is pretty certain. If he had wanted to squeal on Capone, he would have ended up dead anyway. Sorry to say that, Daphne.'

181

She wiped away a tear, and then smiled. 'It's ok. The same thought had occurred to me. Perhaps if he told Capone the ledger existed but that he'd never find out where, the threat would have been enough to keep him alive. Oh, Sandie... you don't think Capone was behind that night in the Green Mill?'

It was a point worth running through my head. Just before it happened James had been acting strangely. But it didn't make too much sense. 'No, I don't think so. Capone wouldn't need to be that devious, and for sure not in his favourite watering hole. I think the sting we unearthed was the truth. It was greed-related, not mob-related.'

'If it was James's life insurance, or part of a plan to bring Capone down, perhaps he hadn't said anything to him yet? Maybe Capone doesn't know about the ledger?'

There was a faint hint of hope in her words. I wished I could have confirmed I felt the same, but my previous experience of the mob eight years ago meant I already knew the new kid on the block was no different to Johnny Torrio, the most powerful kid on the block.

The leaders of the gang always seemed to know what was going on behind their backs, somehow.

I glanced at the worn, black leather-bound ledger, and then at Daphne's worried face. 'I guess it's a faint possibility. But with what's gone down this last week, somehow it seems extremely faint.'

She shook her head, knowing the book burning a hole in the desk was likely the most sought-after artifact in Chicago history. 'We should destroy it, so it doesn't exist anymore.'

I could see the fright that had prompted the words, but it was the worst idea ever. 'Sure, and tell Capone it's gone forever. If he knows it exists, you think he'd believe us?'

'I suppose not.'

'And you think we'd stay alive regardless?'

'I suppose not. We could give it to him, tell him we're not interested.'

'And you think we'd stay alive regardless?'

'I suppose not.'

'Are we in a time-loop here? Daphne, this ledger exists, whether we like it or not. And the fact it's in our possession doesn't bode well for a long life.'

'I suppose... ok, so what do we do?'

I stood up, and walked to the window, as Daphne's shaking hands lit a cigarette. I threw the window open, not just to let the smoke out, but because I needed a few gulps of fresh, cool air.

'Right now, I don't know. It seems every single thing in this bag of crap is connected, and it all leads back to either you or me. Somehow we've got to make it right, before we're not around anymore.'

'Got any suggestions?'

'Not one.'

Daphne moved back to the chair on the other side of the desk. I sat down again, afraid to touch the ledger on the desktop in case it singed my fingers into oblivion.

We couldn't destroy the evidence, because those it implicated wouldn't believe a word of the fact we had. We couldn't hand it over, either to the mob or the tax inspectors, because that would bring about the same end result for us both.

James, and circumstances, had inadvertently made the ledger on my desk untouchable. The phrase "the Holy Grail of Chicago" sprang to mind.

We didn't feel much like eating, but we'd just decided to go and grab Archie and get something for lunch, when we heard a commotion in the tiny reception area. Men were shouting, and a lot of heavy feet were trampling the wooden floor outside the door.

I heard Archie shout, *'You can't just barge in there...'* but his words were in vain. The door burst open, and it became clear we had an unannounced visitor.

The last person on Earth I expected to see in my office.

Chapter 36

It was more than one visitor. The first intruder to appear was Jack McGurn, complete with brandished machine gun, closely followed by two other hoods, equally-well equipped. Then came the man himself, dressed in his usual light-brown coat and matching Fedora.

I'd already realized whoever it was couldn't set eyes on the ledger, but there was little time to react. Unsure where to put it, I resorted to shoving it on my chair seat, and sitting on it.

'Mr. Capone... what a lovely surprise.'

He ignored my totally false greeting, and instantly realized who was in the office with me. 'Well, it's the terrible twosome. And what might you be doing here, *Daphne?*'

She looked at him with the contempt he deserved. 'That's none of your business,' she said, a little hesitantly.

'Everything that goes on in Chicago is my business, lady.' He flicked an arm at her, telling her to vacate the chair. 'Out of my seat.'

Capone or not, I wasn't going to keep my gob shut. 'Actually Scarface, it's my chair, and someone is already sitting in it.'

'Don't call me that... if you know what's good for you,' he hissed. McGurn leveled his gun at Daphne. 'The boss said out, Negro.'

'I beg your pardon?' she said angrily, still not moving. I nodded to her to vacate the seat, knowing our visitors held all the guns. Bravely, and extremely slowly, she did as I advised. Capone sank into the chair, wiping his thick lips with a handkerchief. 'At least someone sees sense. Those goddamn stairs are murder.'

About to tell him he should maybe lose a little weight and keep away from the spaghetti, I decided biting my lip was the better option. Instead I tried to be civil. I almost managed it.

'So what forces you out of your fortress in broad daylight, *Mr. Capone*?'

He didn't seem to like that much. 'Just watch your lip, lady. You know who you're talking to?'

'Your reputation precedes you.'

'Then you know I don't make house calls for just anyone.'

'We are honoured then.'

'No you ain't. We got business, see?' He glanced at Daphne. 'Wasn't expecting to find *that one* here though.'

'*That one* has a name, Mr. Capone. Like the rest of us.'

'Sure. Even though it ain't *her* name anymore.'

'You can refer to her as Daphne. That's a name no one can take away.'

'Whatever. I ain't here to discuss the rights and wrong of names. We got business.'

'I don't do business with the likes of you.'

He sneered at me, in a creepy kind of way. 'Well I got business with you. So let me have it, and I won't allow Jack here to put a bullet in you. Believe me, he's itching to.'

'Um… let you have what?'

'Hey… don't kid a kidder, ok? Especially one who has three guns trained on you.'

He was making a forceful point. But I knew whether I gave him what he wanted or not, neither Daphne nor me were going to see another sunrise. There was no choice but to call his bluff.

186

'Daphne, please let Mr. Capone have it.'

For a second she looked at me in genuine horror, but then clicked into what I was saying. She'd seen me sit on the ledger to hide it, and knew there was only one *it* I could be referring to. She reached into her reticule, as reluctantly as she could pretend to. Then she handed him the necklace.

'You gotta be kidding me.'

He looked at the necklace in his hand, and then threw it on the floor in disgust. I twisted the knife. 'I'm afraid it's not worth as much as it appears. But it'll maybe fetch a couple of hundred dollars.'

'You gotta be kidding me,' he spluttered again.

'Look, Sca... Mr. Capone. I know you've got a heart, hidden somewhere in that ample frame of yours. James put that necklace in the safe deposit box so Daphne wouldn't find it before her birthday. We went to retrieve it, because it's all she has left of him now, after you got him killed.'

'Me? I didn't have nothing to do with that.'

'Sorry, I don't believe you. Obviously Mickey was one of your men.'

'Lady, you're seriously barking up the wrong tree. I didn't have him nullified. And who the hell is Mickey anyway?'

'He's not one of yours then?'

'Geez... you crazy enough to think I'd bother setting it all up in my own speakeasy?'

'Maybe not. But we know someone called Mickey was the killer. I was hoping you could tell me who he is. Daphne wants revenge.'

He glanced up to Jack McGurn, who still looked like he was itching to put a bullet in me. 'You know this Mickey?'

He shook his head, and tightened his finger on the trigger. I swallowed hard. I'd managed to deflect Capone from the real matter in hand, but his right-hand man had a tendency to pull the trigger and think about things afterwards. Our survival still hung in the balance.

'So what else was in the box, Sandie?' Capone asked, getting back to the matter in hand, actually quite politely.

'Nothing. What else would there be?'

He locked his well-proven stare into me, not saying anything for a moment. Somehow, I held the stare. Then he shook his head. 'Knowing devious women as I do, even if you'd found it, it would now be somewhere only either of you would know, am I right?'

'If I knew what you were on about, and if we *had* found it, the fact you're here means it has to be a valuable commodity to you. So yes, it would have been well hidden by now.'

He stood up, and pointed a fat finger at me. 'You better not be sitting on it, Miss Shaw, because if you are, it won't be long until I know.'

I gulped, trying not to let it show. Capone had unknowingly hit the nail on the head, and that particular nail was way too close to my precious bits. 'If we come across it, Mr. Capone, I'll be sure to let you know.'

Jack McGurn looked a little pissed. 'So I can't shoot them then, boss?'

Capone shoved a hand into his shoulder. 'Think thoughts for once, Jack. If you shoot them now, and they have hidden it, we ain't never going to know where it is, are we?'

'Say, maybe if I shoot one of them, it'll make the other come clean?'

Capone shook his head, stood and fastened up his coat. It was at that moment someone decided, perhaps unwisely, to intervene. Archie burst into the room, a handgun in his trembling hands.

'Leave them alone, or you'll have me to deal with...'

188

His bravado didn't last long, three machine guns a bit more persuasive than a single pistol. To be fair, the other two hoods didn't react as quickly as McGurn, who let fly. Archie dived for cover, and somehow managed to avoid the spray of bullets. Capone wrenched McGurn's gun down, but not before he'd let off a few more slugs into the floor.

'For crying out loud, Jack. You so desperate to kill someone you'd settle for a shrimp like him?'

'*Hey…*' Archie began to protest, but then thought better of it.

'Out, all of you…' Capone ordered, knowing the sound of gunfire would likely result in someone calling the police. It wouldn't be a major problem for him, but it would be a nuisance he could do without, in the middle of the day, given the current situation.

In seconds they were gone, clomping down the stairs to a waiting Cadillac Sedan. I watched them go, as Daphne ran to Archie and asked if he was ok. Then we all brushed ourselves down, and tried to brush off a visit that could never be brushed off.

'Thanks Archie, but I think they were just about to go when the cavalry of you arrived.'

'Aw, I couldn't sit back and wait for something to happen, boss.'

Daphne looked impressed again. 'You were very brave, if perhaps a little foolish.'

Archie blushed again, as Daphne gave him a hug.

'Where the hell did you get that gun from, anyway?'

'Um… I've had it since I started working for you, boss. Just in case, you know…?'

'I don't know whether to be impressed or insulted.'

'You'll work it out, boss.'

I didn't get the chance to work anything out. We heard more footsteps on the stairs. Daphne looked at me with fear in her eyes, and Archie's hand tightened on the gun. Then our next visitor arrived. He wasn't very threatening, but he did look very angry.

'Hey Sandie, what the hell? You has clients shooting up the place now? Is not good for business, you know, slugs coming through the ceiling? One customer, he get hole in his burrito.'

'Ouch, Pedro. That sounds painful.'

My little Mexican landlord didn't look too amused. 'You make light of holes in my enchiladas, huh? I tell you, if it happen again, you don' have place to live anymore, ok?'

He stomped back down the stairs, and Daphne grinned at me. 'Maybe making fun of a bullet in the burrito wasn't the best move ever?'

Chapter 37

It likely wasn't the best move ever, but Capone feeling the need to visit us to set out his store was even less amusing. It proved something we weren't sure of; that he'd somehow discovered the ledger existed, and was well aware of the power it held.

It didn't bode well for a peaceful afternoon.

We retreated to the café a couple of blocks down, deciding that avoiding the Mexican restaurant was advisable right then. The red hot ledger was in Daphne's reticule, making sure it didn't leave our sides. We sat around the table like three fugitives, which in a way we were. The safe haven of my office and apartment was safe no more. Capone's organization knew where I lived, and it was a raging certainty he was as worried as hell about what he wasn't sure we possessed or not.

Archie summed it all up, in his own inimitable way. 'It seems to me, boss, that we ain't heard the last of Capone.'

'It seems to me too. But we know now that Mickey isn't part of his organization, whatever use that is to us.'

Daphne shook her head. 'So who is he with?'

'No idea. It might be that he's not with any one gang. There's a new breed of criminal emerging, one who moves between organized gangs, selling information to whoever pays the most for it. Maybe he's an inbetweener.'

'Sounds like a dangerous place to exist.'

'Not a place I'd like to live, for sure. But like police informers, they can be a mine of information.'

'A bit like the ledger.'

I laughed mirthlessly. 'If an inbetweener got wind of that ledger he'd be made for life, as long as he handled it right.'

'Maybe it's good we've got it then.'

Archie groaned loudly. 'Not for us.'

Daphne's eyes clouded into the determined look I was getting to know well. 'Somehow, we've got to make it right, so we can be sure we stay living.'

'How?'

She shook her head again. 'I don't know yet. But there has to be a way.'

'When you work it out, please let me know. I might struggle to sleep at night until you do.'

'I was thinking about that. We have to get out of Chicago, at least for a while.'

'Daphne, that isn't going to alleviate the problem, just postpone it.'

'No, but it might get us a few decent nights' sleep while we think about it.'

The last thing I wanted was to allow Capone to run us out of town, but Daphne was right. The options for a decent night's sleep were becoming severely limited. And if we were going to come up with a plan to get us out of the mess we'd unknowingly fallen into, we needed rejuvenated brains. Her thought was a sound one.

'Shall we get rooms for a couple of nights?'

'I've got a better idea. Well, if you can put up with basic facilities, anyway.'

'If it means I can sleep without getting a bullet in my head, I'll settle for a tent.'

'I can do better. One step better, anyway. You remember I told you James and I bought a beach house? It's in need of renovation, but it's basically sound. We already bought a little furniture, including a couple of beds. We… we were just about to spend the weekends there, doing it up…'

192

She put a hand over her mouth, and I saw her eyes mist over. My heart hit the floor for her again. I wrapped my hand over hers. 'If it's in James's name though, Daphne, they'll find out where we are?'

She pulled herself together. 'No, it's in my name. My maiden name; Ashanti. James said it might be for the best, which made me curious... I know why now.'

'So no one knows about it?'

'No one. It was to be our secret, until it was restored. So perhaps ideal for what we want now.'

'How far out of Chicago is it?'

'Twenty miles up the lake coast, just outside Braeside. It's remote too, our nearest neighbor almost a mile away.'

'No electricity then?'

Daphne smiled. 'Actually, there is. It was the first thing James arranged, so we could work on it after dark.'

My heart was still thumping, on her behalf. 'Oh Daphne, I'm so sorry. But it does sound like an ideal bolt-hole for fugitives.'

'That is what I thought. We should perhaps waste no time, pick up what we need and head there before dark. Then we can regroup, and decide what to do next. You too, Archie. Somehow I fear Mr. Capone already knows where you live too.'

He seemed to be grinning. 'Sure thing, Daphne. I'll tell my mum I'm on a live-in case.'

'In a way you are, Peanut.'

We made our way back to the office. I needed to pick up some files, and a little stuff from my apartment. And Daphne needed the box with a few of her clothes in it. My heart was still on the floor, but my head knew it was a necessary precaution. Apart from Capone himself, Jack

193

McGurn was a loose cannon, kind of literally, who could well take it upon himself to attempt to persuade us to part with our precious possession, in his own unique way.

Nowhere in Chicago was safe for us.

As we reached the sidewalk door, my very real fears were confirmed. The door was open, and judging by the splinters of wood laying on the floor, someone hadn't bothered to pick the lock. I stepped inside the lobby, and listened for sounds to tell me people were still there.

People were still there. The sounds of random ransacking were coming from above. Archie groaned, and started to make for the stairs, pulling his trusty weapon out again. I dragged him back.

'Wait a minute, Wild Bill. It seems Capone didn't take our word for it after all. Daphne, get you and that ledger back to your car, and drive around the block a few times. We can't risk them finding it. Archie and me will go face the music.'

She started to protest, but then realized I was right. One of us needed to protect our primary asset. She put a fearful hand on my arm, and disappeared. I tried to smile to Archie. 'You can go too if you want, Arch.'

'No way. My desk is for sure being ransacked too, and no one does that.'

'Ok, but just keep that gun out of sight, ok?'

'If you insist, boss.'

'I do. No one's losing their life, not today.'

He nodded, and we made our way up the stairs, heading to meet our latest ransackers.

Chapter 38

Archie narrowed his eyes as one of the thugs came into our view, concentrating on pulling his desk to pieces. Despite my warning, the handgun came out straightaway, and aimed at the guy.

'Hey… you better back off. That's my stuff you're wrecking…'

Archie had reacted before I could stop him. The hood reacted too, a little more dramatically. The Thompson sub-machine gun in his hand pointed at us. Then it fired, three rounds which were luckily nothing more than warning shots.

We backed up against the side wall of the upstairs lobby, but both of us knew there was no cover. If he'd chosen to kill us, we were an easy target. But his shots had an effect… the wrecking sounds coming from my office stopped, and a gruff voice shouted out, *'Hey…'*

Someone appeared in the office doorway. Archie pointed his pistol at him, until I pushed his hand down. 'Ok, Archie, I think we're outgunned, don't you?'

He looked at me like he didn't want to accept what I'd said, and I knew if I hadn't pointed out the obvious he would have rushed headlong into the valley of the shadow of death.

You can thank me later for saving your life, Archie.

The guy in the long dark coat and Fedora didn't look too concerned he was about to be attacked by a small platoon codenamed Archie. He didn't look familiar either. But then, as I focused on his craggy, smiling face, he *was* kind of familiar.

I'd never come face-to-face with him before, but I'd seen the odd photo in the newspapers. If I wasn't mistaken it was Albert Kachellek. And knowing who he worked alongside, it was a bit of a surprise to find him in my office. To say the least.

Something was stopping any words coming out of my mouth, but he spoke first anyway. 'Miss Shaw, I assume.' He didn't wait for an acknowledgement to what wasn't a question. 'Now that you're here you can tell us where it is, and save my men wrecking the place any further.'

I glanced through the doorway, and finally found a few words. Two other ugly hoods were inside, waiting on instructions. 'It seems I'm five minutes too late to stop you making it a bit untidy, Albert.'

He laughed, a slightly surprised twang in it. 'You know who I am, I see.'

'Sure. And I know who your boss is too. I'm a little surprised the North Side gang is showing interest in an insignificant private investigator though.'

'Ah, but you see, Miss Shaw, from what Mr. Moran understands, you are no longer insignificant.'

'Well, you can tell Bugs I am in fact totally, utterly insignificant.'

He laughed again, a little unnervingly. 'I think not. So tell me where it is, and we can leave you in peace, to fill in the bullet holes in your lobby.'

I grimaced. The three holes in the lobby walls had just added to the collection I seemed to be making. Pedro wouldn't be too pleased. The latest collection of bullet holes weren't pleasing me either, and neither was the direction from which they'd come. Bugs Moran's Northsiders was the last gang I expected to know about the ledger. It seems good news travels fast.

196

Or bad news, in our case.

Our newest visitor had made reference to the damage he'd inflicted, in order to ram home a very significant point. It wasn't lost on me. But no matter how desperate things seemed, I couldn't give him what he wanted. The reason for the visit was becoming clear. The information the ledger contained was something Capone needed locked away, but his chief rivals wanted the opposite.

Making the contents public to the right people would result in Capone's organization being destroyed, something the North Side gang, his most powerful rivals, would love to see. They would finally be rid of him without a bullet being fired, either in anger or retribution.

The ledger had just become even more of a hot property. And even more likely to get us killed, from one direction or the other. It was even more obvious now that whether or not I gave it up, it would make no difference to staying alive.

'Sorry Albert, but I don't have a clue what you're on about.'

The smile faded, just like that. His eyes narrowed in sudden anger. He turned, and waved a hand to the two men inside my office. They knew exactly what the silent gesture meant.

They let rip, and the room lit up. As the deafening sound of bullets blasting into everything I possessed crashed into our ears, my heart rate hit an all-time high. I watched in horror as the room was destroyed around me. The window glass shattered along with everything else, the random bullets searing through to the street outside.

In ten seconds, my commercial existence was splintered into oblivion. Yet it wasn't the best move my visitor could have made, making it so everyone in close proximity to the building knew they were there. He didn't seem to care... Albert Kachellek wasn't known for his patience, and it seemed I'd found the end of his very short fuse.

As the shooting stopped, he growled menacingly at me. *'Now are you going to tell me where it is?'*

I cringed inside. The guy was close to losing it, and his next bullets would very likely be aimed in our direction. Then, I was saved by the bell.

To be precise, the bells of two police cars, getting louder as they headed down Lawrence. My Mexican landlord must have heard the three shots fired when we first got there, and called the police.

Thank you, Pedro, for saving our lives.

Our visitors didn't seem to want to hang around. As they ran for the stairs, Albert hissed to me. *'I'll be back, lady.'* In seconds they were gone, less than a minute before the police cars pulled up outside.

Frank ran up the stairs, and breathed a sigh of relief as he saw us still standing. I don't quite know what happened then; it seemed I crumpled into his arms, and he held me tight. *'Daphne?'* he asked.

'In... in her car, driving around keeping safe. We found the door smashed in, and then...'

'Ok, ok. You're safe now. What the hell, Sandie?'

I eased myself from him, feeling a little embarrassed at my sudden emotional display. 'Look Frank, the less you know, the better for you. We... we found something, and now it seems everybody and his brother wants it. But we can't give it to anyone, and expect to stay living.'

'Sandie? From what I'm seeing here, you only just stayed living this time.'

198

'Yeah well, thanks to a little Mexican and your intervention. But don't worry, we're getting out of the city for a while. We'll figure it out.'

He cast his eyes at the bullet-ridden wreck of what was once my office. 'Geez, you is treading a fine line here, gal. I don't know if I can protect you.'

'You can't, Frank. We have to figure out a way to protect ourselves. We're going somewhere no one knows about, so we'll be safe for the time being. But we've got to go, right now, before the next visitor comes calling.'

Daphne appeared in the office doorway, a look of relieved horror on her face. 'I heard the gunfire, I was so worried...'

I had to hug her too. 'It's ok. They were too intent on shooting up the office to bother shooting up Archie and me.'

Frank's men were sifting through what was left of my office. The top of my file cabinet seemed to be more holes than cabinet, but the bottom drawer looked to have escaped. If Albert and his men hadn't already found it, Daphne's cash might still be intact.

Then we had another visitor. This one was hardly a surprise. Pedro cast his eyes around the devastation. 'This time you go too far, Sandie. No more, ok?'

'I'm so sorry, Pedro. No, there won't be any more. We're going, and not coming back.'

He shook his head. 'Good. You is not good business no more. And what about damage?'

I shoved him and Frank together, and told them to sort it between them. Daphne and me forced our way through the devastation, and I slid open the bottom drawer of the file cabinet. Albert's men hadn't had the time to find the envelope with the cash. She let out a quiet sigh of relief, and slowly placed it into her reticule.

I grabbed Frank, and tried to smile sweetly. 'Frank, we have to go. One day soon I'll tell you all about it, but for now we have to disappear. I'm sorry, but I'll need to leave you and your good heart to sort this mess out. Is that ok?'

He shook his head. 'Not really, no. But yet again I don't have a choice, do I? I know you got your reasons, I just wish you'd let me help.'

'Trust me, you are helping. I'll be in touch in a day or so, but please bear with being ignorant of the sordid facts until then.'

He lifted his hands from his sides, but we didn't give him any more time to protest. The three of us headed up the stairs to my apartment. We half-expected that door to have been forced too, but it was still locked.

In the realms of small mercies, Albert and his men hadn't had the time to get that far.

Daphne and me grabbed what we could. Getting away was a lot more important that spending a couple of hours deciding what to pack. I already knew I was minutes away from saying a hasty goodbye to the home I'd lived in for eight years, and my father for several years before that.

I grabbed the precious photo of the two of us, and shoved it in a bag with a few of my clothes.

Daphne took my hand, recognizing the emotions running through my heart. 'I'm so sorry it has come to this, Sandie.'

The lump in my throat seemed to be hampering speech, but I managed to mumble a few words. 'Everything comes to an end, Daphne. I'm sorry too, but you and me both need to know I had more than one opportunity to walk away, and I couldn't. So if you want to blame someone, who would it be?'

She shook her head, unable to find the impossible answer. 'We must leave the past behind, Sandie. Take a little time to deal with the present, and then look to the future. We will make it right.'

I couldn't help a wry smile creasing my face. 'Now you're sounding like another Charles Dickens novel. And it's not long until Christmas too!'

She smiled with me. 'Perhaps he was a wise man.'

Archie appeared, Daphne's box of clothes in his arms. 'I hate to break up this meeting of the Dickens appreciation society, but we really should go, you two?'

He was right, as nearly always. I closed the apartment door for the last time, and wiped away a little mistiness. Most of my possessions would have to stay where they were, Daphne's roadster not exactly boasting much luggage space. It might be possible to retrieve what I'd left behind in a few days, but somehow I doubted it.

As I locked the door, gave Frank the key, and hugged him tight, my heart knew it was the end of an era. And as we headed across the road to the car, it knew that nothing was ever going to be the same again.

Chapter 39

Archie called out 'Why do I have to be the one to ride in the dickie seat?'

I turned my head to grin to him. 'Because Daphne and me are in the front seats.'

'Oh, ok... fair point.'

It occurred to me he'd said what he had to distract me from my desolate goodbyes. It was the kind of thing he'd do. And it had worked. As we drove past the Green Mill, and through the streets of the north side of Chicago, I found myself thinking of what we'd find when we got to our destination, not about what we'd left behind.

Then it occurred to me that Daphne had lost a lot more than I had. We'd both been forced into saying goodbye to our homes, but only she had said goodbye to someone she loved.

So far at least.

The suburbs of the city faded away. As we headed in the direction of Milwaukee, our surroundings got a lot greener. We drove by several nice houses, but this area between the two towns was just being developed, and as the next three miles ticked by, there were more trees than houses.

Daphne turned off the road, onto a smaller, dirt road. The light was fading quickly, the tall trees either side of the track casting increasingly dark shadows over us. Archie was keeping a furtive eye behind. We weren't being followed.

The track began to drop downwards a little, and then the lake was in front of us. We threw a left, the track following the shore. It was all quite beautiful, and I began to wish we were there in any other circumstances than why we actually were.

We rounded a slight bend, the trees still shrouding the track on the left side, and then our temporary home was there in front of us. Archie let out a whistle.

'Did you say this was a shack?' he whispered.

Daphne smiled. 'Wait until you have seen the inside, Archie.'

The place was bigger than I expected. Built from wood, and clad in natural timber planks, a slate roof had two dormers rising out of it. A porch that looked like it belonged in the Wild West wrapped around the two sides that faced the lake, clearly there to take advantage of the view.

Even in the fading light, the view was spectacular. Deliberately built just a few feet from the beach, there was an uninterrupted vista of endless water, and little else.

As bolt-holes go, it couldn't have got much better.

We clambered out of the Studebaker, and Daphne slipped the key into the door, which looked in need of a coat or two of paint. We found ourselves in a large, open room, which looked like it was in serious need of a little love. On one wall, a stone fireplace climbed through the roof, an old firegrate sitting in its hearth. A pile of logs was stacked neatly to one side.

Daphne was right though, the place did look structurally sound. As she switched on the electricity and light flooded the space, I could see the layers of dust and sand draping over what little there was in the room. Over on the far side, the space was given over to a small, somewhat ancient kitchen. There was a small electric stove, a few cupboards with old wooden doors hanging off, and little else.

'As I said, one step better than a tent,' Daphne tried to smile. I could see the gloss of tears in her eyes, and took her hand. She and James hadn't spent much time here before his death, but what little they had was clearly bringing back nice but painful memories.

'Remember what you said to me about the past, present and future, Daphne?'

She wiped away a tear, and nodded. 'It is time for me to put that into practice,' she said quietly.

Archie headed to the fireplace. 'I'll make a fire... it's freezing in here.'

An hour later, a huge log fire was warming everything up nicely. Daphne and me had unpacked the two new beds that had never been used, and dusted off the mattresses. It was far too late to assemble the frames, so we swept the floors and put the mattresses straight onto them.

The shack had three bedrooms, but only two beds. Archie raised his eyebrows when we showed him how we'd arranged things, and looked like he was about to suggest he and Daphne shared one of the beds, but said nothing. He was easily intelligent enough to know he wouldn't get very far with that line of thought.

We sat on the threadbare rug we'd placed right in front of the fire, and ate the food we'd picked up en route. The mesmerizing flames warmed us through, and it began to feel a little like school summer camp. Apart from the temperature. And the fact no one was telling us what to do.

Daphne seemed quiet. It wasn't surprising, given the events of the last week or so, and the fact she was sitting by a roaring log fire in her own home without the one person she really wanted. There was little I could say to make that any better, and I sure as hell was wary about saying anything that would make it worse.

So I said nothing, other than complimenting the house, and where it was situated.

'We picked it up for a song. The previous owner died, and his family just wanted rid of it. I don't think they saw the potential.'

'At least you have a little renovation money,' I said, trying to offer some consolation.

She nodded. 'Yes, the cash has been on my mind,' she replied, but didn't elaborate.

'So tomorrow we get cleaning, and make this place ship-shape?'

'I think we need to, don't you?'

A sudden weariness seemed to envelop us, like a fog that unexpectedly rolls in from the lake. By anyone's standards it had been a pretty fraught day, and that was putting it mildly.

Being accosted by two separate gangs of mobsters was an unusual event in anybody's book, the *book* in question suddenly becoming a hotter property than any of us realized. We stood a very good chance of being eliminated by not one but two gangs, and unless we could come up with a way of staying alive, we surely wouldn't.

James in his wisdom had authored the red hot ledger, and in so doing created a Holy Grail that, at its very least, could change the face of Chicago. His ultimate intentions for doing what he did would never be known, but whatever they were, they'd backfired. Because of a necklace that had little real value.

It had ultimately placed the woman he loved in mortal danger, along with Archie and me. James had done all he could to protect Daphne, but hadn't foreseen that an innocent birthday gift had been the catalyst to change all that. We now had a little time in a safe haven to come up with a plan to get ourselves out of that danger, but we couldn't live like fugitives forever.

Something had to happen, and although I hadn't a clue just what that might be, I knew one thing for sure.

It was down to the three of us.

No one else.

Chapter 40

'You any good with wall-building, Archie?

He grinned at Daphne's words. 'Sure I am. I built one at my mum's house, when she wanted to divide one room into two. Why?'

'Because we need to build one, right now.'

I frowned at the conversation. This was news to me, Daphne hadn't said a word about her remodeling plans, and it wasn't really the most important task on our agenda right then. Or was it?

We'd spent the morning cleaning up parts of the house, and assembling the beds properly. Daphne had gone about the tasks in her usual determined way, but she'd been quiet, and a little thoughtful. I'd assumed the emotional turmoil of being in the place she and James had intended making their own was taking its toll, so I hadn't said anything.

We'd eaten the last of our supplies for lunch, and still she was looking like she was somewhere else. I'd just plucked up the courage to ask how she was coping, when she'd thrown the question at Archie. I could almost see the steam coming out of her ears, and was suddenly aware I was wrong about the reasons for her being withdrawn.

Whilst she was grieving for sure, she was also scheming.

She walked over to the start of the kitchen area. 'James and I had planned to build a short wall, to help semi-divide the kitchen area from the living space. It will only be eight feet long, but I think we need to build it right now. The wood and the rest of the materials we need are already in the outhouse.'

'You want me to get on with it now, Daphne?' Archie asked, a curious frown on his brow.

'I think the sooner the better. And if you can, it needs to look like it has always been there. Blend it in to the existing walls, so that it doesn't appear new.'

'I can do that.'

I had to say something... Archie wasn't the only one with a frown on his brow. 'Daphne, what are you scheming?'

'Wait a moment.' She disappeared up the bare staircase, and came back a few moments later with the ledger in her hand. I realized as soon as I saw it what her intentions were. When we'd woken that morning we'd sat side by side in the bed, pouring over its contents. It was just as red hot as we'd thought.

The facts and figures written in its pages were easily enough to bring down Capone, along with a significant number of his known associates. Red hot didn't really do it justice.

Daphne gave the book to Archie. 'Sandie and me have to head to town shortly, but if you would be kind enough to build the wall while we're gone, Archie, I would like you to place this inside the cavity before you attach the exterior panels. Then no one except us will know it is there.'

He nodded, but still looked a little curious. He wasn't the only one.

'Daphne, why are we heading back to town?'

'There are people we have to see, Sandie. Please bear with me... I have a plan to keep us alive. Now, it is time we made our journey.'

It was mid afternoon when we pulled up outside the Wallace and Simpson bank. The sun was heading south as we walked to the main door. Daphne still had the determined look in her eyes, and had found the most elegant clothes in the single box she currently had. There was a thin, sealed envelope in her hand. What it contained, she hadn't revealed to me.

The Dickensian manager looked a little surprised to see us, to say the least. If he did have connections to the mob, he likely wasn't expecting us to still be walking around. Daphne smiled sweetly, and totally falsely, to him. 'I wish to visit my safe deposit box, please,' she said curtly.

He nodded, and we took the trip to the vault again. And once more it looked like he wanted to hang around. Daphne was having none of it. 'Thank you, you may go now. But before you do, I have a question. Do you know my friend, Mr. Al Capone?'

Suddenly he looked seriously embarrassed. 'Um… in a commercial respect, yes. One of his businesses has an account here. More than that I cannot say.'

'No, I don't suppose you can. Your bank holding the legitimate account of a brothel is perhaps not something you want made public knowledge, is it?'

'I did not say it was a brothel, madam.'

'Perhaps not. Now run along, please. We have private business here.'

He scuttled out of the vault, and I grinned at Daphne. 'Really? "Run along"? You've got balls, I'll give you that.'

She slid open the deposit box. 'Perhaps we both have to have, Sandie. It might be our only way to stay alive.'

'Ok, so how did you know the account was for a brothel?'

'I didn't. I still don't for sure, but it stands a good chance. I just wanted to make a subtle point.'

'Subtle?'

209

She smiled, placed the envelope into the box, and slipped it back into its slot. 'We're done here. On to our next port of call, I think.'

'What's in the envelope, Daphne?'

'Later. Time to go and pay a call right now.'

We headed north, still driving to a destination Daphne wasn't revealing. Then as we arrived, I kind of knew why.

'*McGovern's Saloon and Cafe?* This is famous for only one thing.'

'Yes, I know. Bugs Moran's hangout.'

'Are we crazy?'

'I know what I'm doing. Just back me up, and leave the talking to me.'

'Yes ma'am,' I said, only slightly sarcastically.

The man himself was tucking into a feast of chicken and mashed potatoes, his second in command doing the same by his side. Albert Kachallek seemed a little surprised as we sat down on the two spare chairs, but he soon recovered, and looked at us with a sneery grin.

'Can't exactly say I expected to see you here, but it's good you chicks have finally seen sense.'

Daphne matched his sneer. 'Yes... unfortunately it takes a while for us chicks to work out what's best for us, but we usually get there in the end.'

Moran looked like his Christmas had come early. 'So, you handing it over?'

Daphne reached into her reticule like she was, but then smiled sweetly. 'Um... no. But I do have a deal for you.'

Moran growled like a mountain bear. '*Deal?* I don't make deals with dames.'

'Really? I suggest you change that attitude, Mr. Moran, or you might find yourself on a losing wicket.'

210

'Yeah? And what makes you think you hold all the cards?'

'The fact that I do, Mr, Moran.'

He looked like he was about to choke on a piece of chicken. Albert flew to his feet, a handgun appearing from nowhere. 'I'll kill 'em stone dead, right now, boss.'

Bugs Moran slapped him on the arm in a slightly comical way, and then shoved him back into his seat. 'Sit down and shut up, Albert. You're being goofy again. We gotta hear them out first, then kill 'em.'

He let out a slightly unsure smile. 'Sure, boss.'

The big cheese stared at Daphne. 'I take it you have it then?'

'I do,' she said. 'Hidden away, so you'll never find it.'

The sneer got bigger. 'Many have said that before, and regretted it.'

'Ah, but they don't have what I have.'

'So all I gotta do is *persuade* you to tell me where it is, yeah?'

She smiled confidently. 'Let me lay my cards on the table, Mr. Moran. I have a valuable commodity... so valuable in fact, it may never see the light of day again. The only two people who know its location are sitting opposite you right now. And we are both aware that if we tell you where it is, we will lose our lives regardless, either at your hands or Mr. Capone's. So you can do whatever you wish to us, we will *never* reveal its location. Do I make myself clear?'

Bugs glanced to his second-in-command, in a slightly disbelieving way. 'Am I being blackmailed by a dame here?'

'Sure looks like it, boss.'

Daphne played her final card. 'And furthermore, I have set up a small network to ensure our safety. Three of James's trusted friends have been told that if anything happens to Sandie, Archie or myself, the ledger will be sent to the authorities. You will never discover who these three people are, and they do not know what the ledger is or what it contains. They too will never know, unless and until it becomes necessary.'

'So why should I be worried about that?'

'Because my husband was very thorough in what he wrote. For sure it implicates Capone and his organization... but it also implicates the Northsiders.'

'Nah, you're pulling my chain,' he said, but without much conviction.

'Not at all. But in addition, you and Capone are in the middle of a bloody gang war right now. Should it be necessary to pass the ledger to the authorities, they will be told it was *you* who revealed it.'

'So?'

'Come on, Mr. Moran. Capone is already gunning for you, after you almost killed Johnny Torrio. Which backfired on you, because all it did was force him to hand over control to a man far more dangerous than Torrio. He then made your life more difficult. If the Southsiders realize who was responsible for shopping Capone, how long do you think you will stay living?'

Moran pushed his plate away. It looked like he'd lost his appetite. 'So what do you want?'

'When we leave here, we're going to visit Mr. Capone, and inform him of the same facts. What I want is for the two of you to sit down, accept you've been out-manoeuvred, and broker a peace deal. No more gang killings. Nobody wins anyway, except the authorities, who get gangsters eliminated by gangsters themselves. If you do what I ask, and leave my friends and I to live out our lives in

212

peace, I promise you the ledger will never see the light of day.'

'Geez,' they both breathed.

'Do we have a deal, gentlemen?'

'How do I know you're good for your word?'

'You don't. But I can assure you I am, for the sake of being able to go on living my life. You can refuse to believe me, and take drastic action... if you wish to risk such a thing.'

Albert looked like he was itching to reach for his gun again, but Bugs could see the big picture. 'That won't be necessary... or advisable,' he said reluctantly.

Chapter 41

The Windy City was getting dark as we slumped back in the car. We definitely slumped; me with my heart rate going through the roof because I couldn't believe what had just gone down, and Daphne because she couldn't believe it had worked.

'You're a brave lady, I'll give you that.'

She laid her head back on the rest, and closed her eyes. 'Not as brave as I made out, Sandie. My stomach was in knots, and still is.'

'Are we really going to see Capone?'

She nodded, and whispered. 'In a while. I need a strong coffee first.'

I ordered the coffees in the café a couple of blocks away, while Daphne used the phone to make a call. I didn't know who she was calling, but then as she sat down beside me, she revealed all.

'I've just spoken to Tom. He says Capone will be at the Green Mill later, the first time since... that night.'

'Daphne? Surely you're not thinking of going *there* to meet him?'

'I am, yes. You know what they say about getting right back on the horse when you fall off.'

It sounded like a bad idea to me. 'This is a little more than a riding accident, Daphne.'

For a moment her eyes clouded. 'I appreciate that. But I feel like I need closure. Just the once, to walk in there a free woman, do what we have to do, and never go back.'

'I'll say it again... you're a brave woman.'

'Perhaps. But with you by my side, I can do it.'

'Right there beside you, for better or worse. So these three random people, who are they?'

She smiled, the determined look back in her eyes. 'Oh, they don't exist. Just fake bargaining chips, if you like.'

I'd already suspected they were fake, but there was still one more question I had to ask. 'What did you put in the deposit box, Daphne?'

'A piece of paper, in a sealed envelope. A *blank* piece of paper. If as we suspect the manager is being paid off by Capone, if he opens the box with his master key, he will find nothing. A red herring, I believe the phrase is.'

I had to grin. 'Never let me forget how devious you are. A red herring that will leave Capone in no doubt you're not to be messed with...'

'Exactly.'

We stayed in the café for over an hour, talking about everything that was unrelated to the matter in hand, and then made our leisurely way to North Broadway. We sat in the car opposite the Green Mill, waiting for the time Capone and his crew would arrive.

Another hour passed, and then just as a little snow began to settle gently over the road, the man himself turned up. This time there was no entourage other than a few bodyguards, and he slipped inside quietly, leaving two armed security men at the door.

'Game on,' Daphne said quietly.

We gave Capone five minutes to settle in, then walked across the road, and as we expected, came up against a brick wall. 'Sorry ladies, no one's allowed in right now.'

Daphne gave the men her dazzling smile. 'Oh, I think Mr. Capone will want us to be let in. Please tell him Daphne deMountford is here to see him. *Now, please?*'

215

I had to smile. The hoods looked at each other like they couldn't quite believe what had hit them. Then one disappeared inside, doing what the force of nature called Daphne had commanded.

Two minutes later he was back, still looking a little bemused. 'You can go in,' he muttered.

Daphne hesitated as we walked through the foyer. I took her hand. 'You ok?'

She nodded. 'Yes. It is perhaps a little harder than I was telling myself. But we have a job to do.'

Yet again I found an overpowering kind of admiration for her. She wasn't just about to play one of the most devious men in Chicago, but she was doing it in the place where her husband had been killed a little over a week before.

It took the kind of courage I knew I didn't possess.

Tom was behind the bar as we walked in. He didn't look surprised to see us; Daphne had clearly told him on the phone we would be coming. He did look a little nervous though. Daphne kept her head up as we strode over to Capone's booth, not looking anywhere except right at him.

He didn't seem that surprised either, although he pretended to be. '*Daphne*... you're the last person I expected to see in here, for sure.'

We sat down on the curved seat, and she smiled sweetly. 'I suppose I have a confession to make, Mr. Capone.'

He was no fool. 'So you do have it then.'

'I do. But you won't ever find it.'

'You sure about that, lady?'

'Oh yes. And it appears there is a mole in your organization. No doubt you know Bugs Moran is also aware

216

of the existence of the ledger. We've just been to see him, and told him what we're about to tell you.'

He glanced to Jack McGurn, sitting to his right. 'That explains the phone call, then.'

'Bugs been in touch, Mr. Capone?'

'A couple of hours ago. He's coming here later, says he wants a meet.'

'I suppose I'd better tell you why then.' Daphne gave him the same spiel she'd given Bugs, except she put more emphasis on the incriminating facts, from Capone's point of view. He sat back, trying to appear unconcerned, sipping his gin as he listened to the words that he really didn't want to hear. She finished with the same question.

'So do we have a deal, Mr. Capone?'

He glanced to Machine Gun again, who scowled at us with his evil black eyes, but couldn't seem to find any words. Capone threw his hands in the air. 'I guess right now you hold all the cards, much as I hate to admit a dame is getting one over on me.'

'It is not me. This is down to my husband, who has in effect stitched you up, and paid the price with his life. I am simply trying to make sure his final wish, which is that I live in peace, is honoured. Will you honour that, Mr. Capone?'

'Do I have a choice?'

'Not if you wish to stay in control, no.'

He sank the dregs of his shot. 'It seems you're being honest with me, Daphne. So I'll be honest with you. I'm tired of this tit-for-tat, eye-for-an-eye stuff. Good men on both sides are losing their lives, for no real goddamn reason. Maybe this little kick in the ass of yours is what our organizations need. If Moran is willing to call a cease-fire, then so am I.'

McGurn didn't seem to like that very much. 'Boss...'

217

'Sure, I know your itchy trigger finger ain't gonna be thrilled by that, Jack… but think about it a moment. Just what is your life expectancy right now, huh?'

He went quiet, thinking about it for a moment.

Daphne needed a definitive answer. *'So do we have a deal?'* she repeated herself.

Capone shook his head. 'Sure. As long as Moran is genuine when we meet later, then you got a deal.'

'Oh, he will be genuine, trust me.'

Capone waved a slightly-annoyed hand at us. 'Now get outa my sight. I don't want to set eyes on either of you ever again, see?'

We left, walking out of the joint with our heads still up. As we crossed the road to the car, I noticed Daphne wipe away a tear. It had been far harder for her than she'd let on, which wasn't exactly unexpected. As we closed the car doors she finally let go of the bravado, holding me tight and sobbing wretchedly on my shoulder.

I let her cry it out, but I had to tell her how I felt. 'That's closure taken care of. Now you need to keep hold of the fact you're the bravest woman I've ever met.'

Chapter 42

Archie had been his usual star when we got back. The new wall was made, and the ledger firmly buried inside where no one without a sledgehammer could get to it.

Daphne gave him a hug, which in Archie's mind was worth every minute of the work, and then she took us outside. The snow clouds had gone, and a bright moon cast a pillar of yellow light across the gentle waters of the lake. It was freezing cold, but quite beautiful.

We walked across the beach, right up to the surface of the water. Then she held something up in her hand, her misted eyes gazing thoughtfully at the tiny object that had caused so much upset, and changed so many lives.

The safe deposit box key glinted in the moonlight as she finally found a smile. 'All I have left of James is now a part of this house, and I pray it always will be. But now, this innocuous little thing is never going to cause anyone any grief again. Small and insignificant though it is, making it disappear forever is the final closure I need.'

I knew then what our vigil was all about. '*Do it, Daphne,*' I whispered.

She arched her long arm backwards, and threw it as hard as she could. A hundred yards out in the lake, we heard the gentle plop as it hit the surface, and disappeared forever.

The next morning it was time for Archie to return to his mother. We all knew it was safe for him to go back to Chicago, now the incredibly-brave Daphne had included him in her staying-alive deal.

I told him I would be in touch in a few days, and put a small wad of cash in his hand to tide him over. Part of me

219

wondered if I would ever be able to employ him again; if I would ever have the means to be a private investigator any more. I had no office and no home, so my personal future wasn't exactly looking bright.

Daphne asked if I would remain at the house, saying there were a few things that needed doing there, and that Archie deserved a ride in the front seats anyway. I had to agree he did, but I still found her request a little curious, especially as she said she might be some time, and would be going shopping for supplies on the way back.

I watched them drive away, not too unhappy I would be on my own for a few hours. A little solitude would help me get my head around what my immediate future held, and maybe an idea about where it might happen.

By the time Daphne got back four hours later, I hadn't got very far with possible futures. There just didn't seem to be many options. I'd tangled with the mob, and not come out of it very well. Sure, Daphne's crafty plan had ensured we would all be left alone from now on... but left alone to do what?

I'd been kicked out of my wrecked office and my home, and run away with very little to show for it. Unless I could find a new place to live and work, with severely limited resources, my prospects weren't looking too good.

I'd started to feel a little on the depressed side, until I remembered I wasn't the only one who'd suffered loss. Daphne had her beach home, but it needed a lot of work and money to get it to a decent standard.

But she no longer had the man she loved. And that was a more sobering thought than anything else.

We unpacked the shopping together. I told her of my thoughts while she'd been gone. She didn't seem that surprised by them.

'I will confess I've been thinking the same things.'

'Yes, but at the end of the day you've lost something that was a lot more precious than anything I once had.'

She stopped unpacking, and smiled to me. 'Sandie, the past is gone. The present only lasts but a moment in time. Perhaps now we need to look to the future.'

'That's what I was doing while you were gone. But I confess I don't seem to have got very far.'

'Then let me kick-start it for you.' She threw her eyes to the ceiling, like she was summoning up the courage. 'Sandie, I would like you to live here with me… permanently.'

I turned away, unwilling for her to see the mistiness in my eyes. 'Daphne, that's very generous. But I think you've already done enough for me.'

'Please, it is not so generous. This place needs a lot of work, and I don't think I can find that determination on my own. And… and apart from that…'

'Daphne?'

'It is a selfish thing, but I don't wish to live alone, Sandie.'

I turned back to her, and pulled her into a hug. 'In that case, how could I not help my best friend out?'

The next day, my best friend sprang another surprise on me. After lunch, she suddenly announced we were driving back to the city.

'Am I allowed to ask why?'

'Um… I need to collect a few more of my things from the precinct, and also we should go to your old apartment, and

221

see if any of your stuff is still there. I will not take no for an answer from Mexican landlords, Sandie.'

'I bow to your authority, sir.'

She smiled, but as we set off, her slight hesitation when I'd asked why we were going to the city hadn't gone unnoticed. I got the feeling she was up to something, yet again. And yet again, she wasn't telling me what it was.

Our first port of call wasn't on the list I'd been made aware of. I found myself on the sidewalk in front of James's office building.

'Come along,' my chauffeur instructed.

I followed her into the elevator to the fourth floor, and along the passageway I'd travelled once before. This time though, I was met by a new office door, and it sure hadn't been forced open. It reminded me of my old office door; half-glazed, with words etched into the glass. I stared at it, trying to persuade my eyes to convince my brain what they were actually seeing.

The lettering was very elegant, but the words were a bit of a shock...

deMountford and Shaw, Elite Private Investigators

I could only mumble the words, somewhat inanely. 'Um... shouldn't it be Shaw and deMountford?'

Daphne laughed. 'I thought about that. But don't you think it sounds better the other way around?'

I had to admit it did. '*Elite?*' I mumbled again.

'I still have a few connections. I'm already organizing some advertising in the newspapers, to target the right people. If that's ok of course?'

'I... this is a bit of a shock, Daphne. I... I suppose so.'

222

'Would you like to see inside? Someone's been busy.' She eased the door open. The someone shouted out as he saw us. 'Boss! Sorry, bosses!'

'Archie?'

'How you doing, Boss One?'

'A little taken aback, if I'm honest.'

'Aw, boss. Look, three desks, one for you, one for Daphne, and one for me. How cool is that?'

I managed to turn my head, and look inquisitively at a grinning Daphne. 'I take it you and Archie have been colluding behind my back then?'

'I suppose we have, yes. Because of me you lost your office and your home. James's office is paid every six months in advance, and he'd only just made the next installment. It would be such a shame to waste it...'

'So are you saying you want to become a private investigator... with us?'

'I feel the need, yes. I have developed a taste for fighting injustice now... and there is unfinished business anyway.'

'There is?'

'There is. We still don't know who killed my husband.'

'She has a point, boss,' Archie quipped.

I found my head shaking again, still trying to get itself around what was going on. 'You really are sneaky, aren't you?'

'You complaining?'

'No. Just keep reminding me which one of us is the devious one.'

———

We hope you enjoyed Sandie's first adventure, 'Murder at the Green Mill'. We would be eternally grateful if you can spare two minutes to leave a review on Amazon. It really is very easy, and makes a huge difference; both as feedback to us, and to help potential readers know what others thought.

Thank you so much!

A fascinating footnote from Richard…

Those of you who already know our work will be aware we like to blend fact and fiction in our stories. This is particularly true with Sandie, as you will have seen.

One lesser-known true fact of the time the book is set, is that a truce was actually agreed between the Capone and Bugs Moran organizations. No one was ever sure why the truce was agreed… but now you've read the book, maybe you know!

The cease-fire lasted for quite a while, during which time no mobsters were killed by mobsters. But eventually, and inevitably, it broke down, and the killings began again. It culminated in one tragic and famous incident, which truly shocked America.

'The St. Valentine's Day Massacre' was an ill-conceived act by Capone to eliminate Moran (who by a stroke of pure chance, escaped being harmed). It was the spark that led to Capone's downfall.

More about that in future Sandie books!

Look out for Sandie's next adventure – 'Christmas in Chicago is Murder'
It's coming in time for your stocking!

If you like Sandie, you'll love Daisy...
Check out her first adventure –

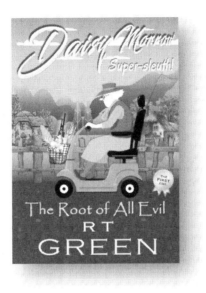

The Daisy Morrow series is now six books old... soon to be seven!

Read about Sandie, Daisy, and everything else on our website – rtgreen.net

AND DO COME AND JOIN US

We'd love you to become a VIP Reader.

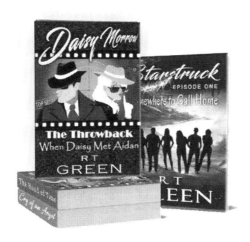

Our intro library is the most generous in publishing!
Join our mail list and grab it all for free.
We really do appreciate every single one of you,
so there's always a freebie or two coming along,
news and updates, advance reads of new releases...

Go here to get started...
rtgreen.net

Printed in Great Britain
by Amazon